ELEMENTAL ARCANE

THE ELDRITCH FILES
BOOK ONE

CALDWELLPRESS.COM

Published by Caldwell Press
Cover Design © 2014 by Lou Harper

Thank you for purchasing and reading Elemental Arcane. It would be greatly appreciated if you could take a moment and leave an honest review of this novel within the guidelines of your favorite retailer.

QUALITY CONTROL: If you find typos or formatting problems, please contact ph8dra@comcast.net so they may be corrected.

If you want to be notified when Phaedra's next novel is released and get free stories and occasional other goodies, please sign up for her mailing list at her website, phaedraweldon dot com.

Your email address will never be shared and you can unsubscribe at any time.

As always, for my father.

This rough magic I here abjure and when I have required some heavenly music, which even now I do, to work mine and upon their senses that this airy charm is for, I'll break my staff, bury it certain fathoms in the earth, and deeper than did ever plummet sound, I'll drown my book.

William Shakespeare, *Hamlet*

Eighteen Years Ago…

"You leave this house *tonight,* of all nights," George Hawthorne sliced his hand sideways through the air to emphasize his resolve. "And our marriage is over."

Crisp October wind moved the trees outside the kitchen window behind his shoulder, heralding a rain of orange, yellow and red leaves as they struck the glass with a delicate tapping in the silence that followed her husband's declaration.

Elizabeth "Eliza" Hawthorne faced the love of her life, her husband, the father of their smart, beautiful and precocious child sleeping in her room upstairs. Eliza squared her shoulders at the threat and made sure her expression was determined, but not angry. If she had to find a word to describe how she felt at that moment, she would say resigned.

The kitchen table separated them. George stood in front of the sink washing dishes, as he always did after dinner, and Eliza just inside the kitchen door, dressed in her day-job clothing. A pantsuit, boots and her Smith & Wesson strapped to her side. What he didn't see were the ritual robes in the bag at her feet, along with everything she and her coven needed to rid themselves of an evil that had entered their world.

Eliza took in a sharp breath and allowed her shoulders to rise. "It's work, babe. I caught a case and I have to go check it out."

"Can't Boudreaux take it on his own? You're getting death threats—and don't deny it. I saw them, Eliza."

"I can't do that, George. *I'm* well aware of what's threatening me, but I can't risk my partner's life when he doesn't know what's out there."

George made a rude noise as he put his hands on his hips. "Can't you put a protection spell on him with your hocus pocus and just stay home? Safe? With your family? Tonight, of all nights? Even I know that wind out there isn't natural, and Halloween's the worst night to be out, especially with a full moon. There's a lot more crazies out there than usual."

Hocus pocus. That was his name for what she could do. Eliza wasn't angry with him, because she knew how scared he was. There was something out there hunting her, because she'd been hunting it. What she was and what she did sometimes frightened him as well.

Eliza had been born a God Mother's child, a daughter of Diana, a Little Bender.

A Witch.

It was written in Eliza's blood, scrolled within the very cells of her being, and not something she could turn on and off at a whim. For eleven years she explained it to him, and when their daughter was born eight years ago, he asked if their little Samantha was a Witch as well. Eliza was honest with him. "She has the same Gifts that I do, and that my mother had before me. She will be a Witch of the Elementals."

Her family had celebrated this, to have three Witches born with the most rare of Gifts. A daughter to a mother, as Eliza's mother had been. Three generations of Elemental Magic.

Elementals were guardians in a sense, protecting mankind from creatures born to do evil. Eliza had chosen to serve in law enforcement to fight evil on the human front, and graduated at the top of her class, even as a detective. Now her search for an ancient, sickening darkness had come to fruition and tonight that evil would be removed.

Exorcised with a kind of magic the God Mother's children were forbidden to use.

Eliza had accepted the responsibility such a thing could carry and had prepared for whatever punishment the Magical Parliament might force upon her, but she was prepared for however the magic would change *her*. Because this magic was born in the realms past their own. This magic held the secrets of life and death itself.

The Magic of Arcane.

No Witch that used it, unless tainted with the blood of the Demon Realms, could wield it without a price.

Because of this, because Eliza didn't know if she would change or the magic would take its price from somewhere else, she'd safeguarded her family in case she didn't return in the same way she departed.

It was a way to protect them. It was the *only* way she knew how.

"I can't. This thing that's threatening me isn't something I can protect people from anymore. It's something I'm going to have to deal with, but not through law enforcement. I've searched for it for three years, both as a detective and as Mother's Tracker." She didn't use her official title within the coven often, but tonight it seemed fitting. "This evil has used up bodies, destroyed families and towns through the centuries. It tried to possess a politician just last month, but luckily I scryed what that evil was doing and we stopped it, we ran it down. Soon we'll send it back to where it belongs, okay? When the time is right. But tonight I have to do my job."

She surprised herself at how easy it was to lie to her husband. She and her coven hadn't just run the evil down; they'd taken it and locked it in a hole to weaken it, where it couldn't feed on blood and couldn't call for help. Tonight was the night the ritual had to be done. Tonight, when the veil was thinnest between their world and the Demon Realms.

Eliza hated lying to him, but she didn't want him to worry, and she didn't want to worry their daughter. Once this thing was exorcised, and everything went well, they could get back to their life of simple things, like baking brownies and book fairs at the school, and the impending Thanksgiving cooking marathon at the end of next month.

If the Magical Parliament chose to sentence her for using Arcane Magic, Eliza assumed the worst they could do was warlock her, a means of banishing her from the coven and sealing her power. She could accept anything as long as it meant she kept her family.

The windows creaked as the wind kicked up, blowing heavier items like twigs and branches against the glass as if to emphasize her declaration of justice. Eliza didn't feel as confident as she had before George confronted her. There was something ill about the weather, coming so quick and cold on All Hallow's Night. In Mississippi, the cold shouldn't be there before December.

She moved around the table to put her hands against the sides of her husband's face. "I'll be back before daybreak. Sam has her play tomorrow night for All Souls. Do you have the camera battery charged?" Magical energy played havoc with some modern conveniences.

Her husband, her love and her world, finally smiled at her. Worry and concern filled his eyes as he slipped his hands around her waist. "Yes," he said, though his voice was muffled because he buried his face in her neck. "I love you, Elizabeth Hawthorne."

Eliza's eyes burned as he pulled back and looked into her face. She searched his handsome features and hoped the price of the magic would not be her eyesight. She would miss seeing his stunning blue eyes, the same color their daughter possessed. "I love you, George Hawthorne. Here and in the Summerlands." It was how she always parted company with him.

The wind whipped her hair about as she stepped outside, bag on her shoulder, and closed the door behind her. Leaves and debris tumbled over the cold ground as she checked to make sure the house was locked and then held out her hand to check the wards and initiate the safeguards she'd put in place. A webbing of pentagrams flashed a bright white at her touch and she gave them a quick jolt of her Spirit to lock the spell. Her family's lives and their thoughts continuing as if she were a suspended memory.

If she returned, she could unlock the spell and life would continue. And if she didn't unlock it, then…

The wind changed against her back and she turned.

Her Bronco was parked at the end of the driveway, ready for Eliza to back out without disturbing her sleeping daughter. She opened the SUV's hatchback and set her bagged supplies inside. When she closed the back door, the wind shoved her hard against the SUV. The whip and curl of it took her breath away as leaves stuck to her jacket and pants. Several seconds passed before she realized it wasn't the wind that held the leaves to her suit, her skin, her face and her hair. She pulled at a large yellow leaf on the back of her hand.

To her horror, the leaf pulled her skin with it and left behind a raw, bleeding wound.

More leaves slapped against her with harder force. She held up her arms to protect her face as they fused themselves to her hands, binding her fingers together. More leaves wrapped around her legs, individually and then together as they bound her ankles and she fell on her side and rolled down the driveway, unable to stay upright and fight the push and pull of the maelstrom.

The leaves moved and crawled about her as they sought out the uncovered parts of her. Eliza whispered the words for Fire, summoning her power. Several of the leaves ignited, but they burned her as well and she screamed in pain as she rolled on the ground in an attempt to smother the magical fire.

Eliza soon found herself bound from head to toe in an autumn prison of yellow, brown, red and orange leaves. They covered her mouth, fused her lips together, and kept her quiet. The only parts of her left uncovered were her eyes, her nose and her ears.

A buzzing noise filled the night, drowning out the sound of the winds and she thought of a million bees. Eliza panicked, thinking something had summoned a farmer's hive to sting her while she lay helpless.

But that's not what she saw. Eliza realized the leaves had been focused to leave her eyes uncovered so she could see what was coming for her.

Down the road of her subdivision thundered horses. Nine in all. Their hooves were made of white fire and she wasn't sure if they were truly striking the ground even though it vibrated beneath her. A woman adorned in gleaming silver, seated on a white horse whose silver caparison flashed with moonlight, was the group's focal point and led them to where Eliza lay.

Wolves materialized out of a thick mist that formed around Eliza. She made protesting noises and squirmed as she tried to roll away. The wolves, large and magnificent, in hues of gray, black and white, surrounded her and nudged her back into their center with their snouts.

They parted as the woman on the white horse inched her beast forward. Eliza looked up into the most beautiful of faces. She was as pale as the moon, with hair as dark as midnight, and lips the color of blood. Her gown moved with the colors of winter, pale blues, whites and grays. The fabric looked as if it were made of ice.

When she dismounted from her stallion, her feet never touched the ground, but floated atop the mist.

"Elizabeth Alexandra Hawthorne," the woman said in a voice that was both commanding as well as luxurious and seductive. "You've made someone very, *very* angry at you. So they've asked me to make sure you don't do that again."

Angry? What? Who? She tried to ask questions but the pain of trying to pry her raw and bleeding lips free of the leaves prevented her.

"Aww…" the woman said as she knelt down. So close, Eliza could see the woman's skin was as smooth and flawless as marble. Ethereal. And her pale ears parted her ebony hair in long, elegant points.

Faeries! No!

"Now, there's no need for you to talk anymore, Elizabeth. No need to worry or think ever again. Your enemy gets what they want, and I get what I want," she smiled, showing rows of sharp teeth. "I get another God Mother's child of my very own."

Eliza screamed as the pain from the leaves covering her intensified. She heard the fabric of her suit sizzle and saw smoke rise from beneath the leaves to mingle with the Faerie mist. She felt the searing burn of her flesh as it melted, and heard the crack of her bones as they mutated inside of her. She writhed and rolled around as her thoughts darkened and simplified and she knew the name of the woman. The name of her new master.

Medbh. Queen of the Unseelie Sidhe.

Soon the pain faded and she could stand on all fours. When she raised her head, she stood as high as the horse's shoulder. And when she felt something touch her side, she looked into the sad eyes of another wolf.

Welcome, sister, came the voice in her mind. It softened the transition from being human to wolf for Eliza. But it didn't replace the sadness.

As Medbh remounted her stallion and urged her wolves on, Eliza looked back at the house as all memories of her loving husband and little girl faded away.

The wolf howled and joined her new pack as the Faerie Queen continued on her wild hunt with one more hunting beast.

ONE

"He's late."

I ignored Kyle's irritating need to state the obvious and pointed to the black band on his left arm. "What's with that? Some royal thing?" Kyle was a bit of an anglophile.

"I'm in mourning for Jeremy."

"Jeremy?"

"The guy I met at Lord Siril's party on Saturday. Don't you remember? The one with the puppy dog eyes?"

"What, did he die? Hence the armband?"

"Just in my heart. I saw him with a hottie last night at *Le Roundup*."

I sighed. No wonder he was pointing out my boyfriend's shortcomings. Kyle was suffering from a broken heart.

The fourth one of the week.

We were in my magic shop, *Bell, Book and Candle*. It sat sandwiched between an ice cream parlor and a tourist bookstore, and it was a block or so down from Lafitte's Blacksmith Shop and Bar on Bourbon Street, New Orleans, Louisiana. We were close enough for tourists to meander in and buy the gitchie-goomie harmless crap that wouldn't even screw up their karma, visible to our legitimate clientele of the magical persuasion, and far enough away from the crazy drunks of Bourbon Street, which was my preference.

Wednesdays were slow. It's that middle-of-the-week slump where customers are tired and Friday feels too far away. A few tourists meandered in and out, but they mostly came through for the atmosphere. Kyle Kendrick, my closest friend and my partner in this life of shop keeping, maintained what he called ambiance, with burbling desk fountains, quiet dulcimer music that gave me a righteous headache, and the oh-so-not-subtle fog machine he pulled out every Halloween to give the place that Other World feel.

Both hands on the clock over the front door pointed straight up. Noon. I was waiting on Robin, my boyfriend of six months, to pick me up for our usual Wednesday lunch. There was a killer taco place just a mile up the street on St. Philip that made the best burritos, so I always treated.

He'd called earlier and said a few roads were blocked off, so getting through traffic to my shop would be iffy. I knelt down beside Grey, my wolf familiar, and stroked her soft, white and gray fur. I didn't really know if she was a familiar, but from the moment she showed up in Macon, Georgia during one of my trips, and helped me escape a grave-guarding party of whacked-out cultists bent on sacrificing me on the altar of their declared freedom, I considered her my *bestest* friend in the whole world.

Sort of telling, isn't it, that my best friend is covered in fur and walks on all fours.

And is a girl.

It tells me I need to get out more.

I considered heading back into my office to catch any news on the roadblocks.

That's when something thudded hard against the front window.

Grey and I looked up from where we knelt near the front to see a woman splayed against the glass. My shop had four tall windows, two on either side of the door. She was at the window on the left, closest to the entrance. Blood covered her wide-eyed face. It smeared over the glass in long streaks as she pawed at the window and I could see it splattered over her clothes.

This wasn't how our usual mornings started at the shop, but it wasn't completely surprising either since normal had never been a stable part of my life. That's because I'm Samantha E. Hawthorne, local Witch and entrepreneur.

"Great Lord and Lady!" Kyle dropped the tarot deck he'd been arranging on a nearby table that held up a burbling desk fountain, and ran to the door. Grey and I stood as Kyle pulled the bloody lady inside.

Something smelled wrong. And I don't mean like a bad smell. I mean *wrong*. The smell wasn't part of this world, but somewhere else. Maybe *something* else. Grey gave a low *gruff* growl. She smelled it too. The only way to describe it to anyone who wasn't Gifted with magic would be raw chicken, left in a warm, sealed room. For a week.

The woman went down on her knees, grabbing at Kyle's shirt. Her gaze locked with his. "Call nine-one-one! It's my daughter! My daughter!"

Oh Lady Darksome…is the blood her daughter's? This was bad, bad news and I was glad the meandering tourists had long since left. I knelt next to Kyle and put my hand on the woman's arm, somewhere that wasn't covered in blood. I needed to use my *dex* spell for a species check. It worked a lot like a pokédex in that it allowed me to analyze people and discover *what* they were. Human, Lycan, Vampire or Other.

And Other wasn't always the better choice. In fact, it *never* was. I needed to know if her daughter had been attacked, *she* wasn't the attacker.

Usually Other creatures, meaning things that weren't part of this world, could sense me and what I was. They knew I had the power to banish their asses back to where they belonged, and I could do it painfully. I used a small version of the spell, like *dex* lite. It didn't require any words or singsong incantations. Just me with a desire to find out if she was human.

Anyone with magical or Other sight could see my magic the way I did. Concentric pentagrams appeared one after the other, each with their corresponding Element. An Earth banishing, a Water banishing, a Fire banishing and an Air banishing. The last would be the Spirit summon and I would have my answer.

She was human.

But that *smell*…

"Hey, did you guys hear about what happened over at the— what's going on?" Ivan Westerfield, a friend, employee and a member of my little group, or coven if you like the word, though we were way less than the recommended standard of thirteen, came around my right side, probably from the break room. He instinctively locked the front door and faced us as Kyle and I knelt with the bloodied woman.

Ivan wasn't like anything or anyone I had ever known. He defied all stereotypes, from his Japanese American features, to his grunge face piercings and body tattoos to his German English name and southern accent.

But it didn't stop there. Ivan was a Witch like no one had ever seen.

And I mean *no* one.

"*Balls*…is that blood?" Ivan moved around and crouched next to me. The light from the windows glinted off the silver ring in his lower lip. He moved the woman's hair from her neck and tucked it behind her ear, exposing what looked like bite marks, as well as a missing chunk of skin. The coppery scent of blood mingled with that foul odor. "What is that smell?"

I knew Ivan would sense the *wrong* about this whole thing. "Ivan, call an ambulance."

"My way or—"

"The *fastest* way." Ivan's way was the most unconventional method of making a call. I addressed the bleeding woman. "Ma'am, did the same person who attacked you, also attack your daughter?"

The woman moved her left hand from Kyle's arm and put her *Kung-Fu Death Grip* on my arm. "No! My *daughter* attacked me! My daughter did this and then she jumped on that nice grocery man!"

Whaaaaat?

TWO

Her *daughter?*

The three of us glanced at each other, unsure what to say. I just wanted to make sure *I* heard her right.

Her daughter attacked her? And a grocer?

I've never been a comforting person. It's just not in my nature. Luckily, Kyle was and he reached over to wrench the woman's hand from my arm. *Ouch.* That was going to leave a bruise.

Kyle soothed the woman while my brain ran at a breakneck speed. Was this lady for real? How old was her daughter? Was she small or large? What the hell possesses a daughter to bite her mother? Was it a disease? Or was the girl maybe possessed by a demon?

I stood up with an eye on the front windows. The million-dollar question?

Where was her daughter *now?*

"You don't look so good," Ivan said as he stood with me.

My gaze roamed over the blood on the glass, the floor and now on my shirt. "I'm trying to figure out what would have caused a girl to just viciously attack her mother like that. *And,* figure out where her daughter is at this moment." I focused on Ivan. His light brown eyes calmed my nerves, much like Robin's usually did. "We need to find out if someone called the police. Can you do that? Did you call an ambulance yet?"

"Doing it now." Ivan closed his eyes, took several deep breaths, and held his hands out, palms up. I could see him login to the web as the air between he and I shimmered and a smattering of ghostly screen images appeared. His eyes opened, no longer brown, but green. His hands moved over invisible connections only he could see, broke into security cameras and tapped their way into the computer systems of the local New Orleans police department.

This is what made him so unique.

Ivan was a Cyber Witch. He manipulated the magic of the electronic world. The thing that usually threw a wrench into the use of magic with its magnetic fields was his playground.

See? What'd I tell you? Like nothing anyone's ever seen.

"Please…you've got to stop her before she kills someone else."

I looked back at the woman as Kyle put his hand to the side of her face. A soft, yellow glow ringed the outline of his hands and I sensed his calming magic cover the woman in layers of peace. But I also knew silencing the woman's hysteria was like putting a Band-Aid over a meteor crater.

It just wasn't gonna work.

And then… "Wait," I held up a hand. "Kills someone else? Your daughter killed someone?"

The woman looked up at me. "Mr. Higgins."

Well crap on a dragon's— "So, you were in Mr. Higgins's grocery store when she attacked you?"

The lady nodded as Kyle concentrated on keeping her hysterics under a short lcash.

"And…you ran here?"

"Yes."

"Why here? That grocery is two blocks down."

"I'm so sorry but something pulled me to your door. I knew you could help me."

Kyle opened his eyes and looked up at me. "Yeah…that Guardian Sentinel thing of yours at work again."

Crap.

Grey growled as she leapt past me to the door. She stood in front of it, her four legs splayed out as if she were positioning herself for a fight. Her lips drew back, exposing some seriously sharp fangs.

"Baby...what's wrong..."

A little girl, no more than six, maybe seven, ran up to the window at that moment and slapped her hands flat against the same glass. More blood spattered from the impact over the slick surface. I felt, as much as sensed, the abominable evil that radiated from her and took several steadying steps back.

And the smell...this thing is what smells so bad!

"Holy Goddess...what the hell *is* that thing?" Kyle asked, noticing the little girl at the window (and who wouldn't?). That slip broke his concentration with the mother. She turned and threw up her hands as she cried out in terror when she spotted her daughter.

Dressed in pink corduroy pants, a Hello Kitty shirt and pink jacket, the girl clawed at the glass, and then slammed it with her fists. Her eyes glowed red, and when she opened up her mouth she exposed rows and rows of sharp little teeth.

Uh uh. I'm sorry. But that just ain't right. It sure as hell looks familiar...where have I seen this before?

I had no idea what it was or where it came from, but I sure as shit planned on putting it back. This wasn't this woman's daughter anymore. "Kyle, strengthen the wards."

"Already on it." He stood, pulling the hysterical woman with him to the back of the shop. He would probably lock her in my office so he could get to his thurible, mortar and pestle. Kyle was a Hedge Witch, a Little Bender who could do exactly as the legends said; bend and shape reality by using natural combinations of herbs, spells, incantations and symbols. My Elemental Magic allowed me speed and strength, but Kyle's would last longer with little effort exerted from his own personal energy. His magic came from organic things around him.

I held up my right hand to feed energy into the wards until I felt Kyle's power kick in and appreciated the faint aroma of Dragon's Blood Rede as it softened the stench of the thing in the window. The ward should stop the little monster from getting *into* the shop, even if it broke the glass.

"They're on their way," Ivan said from where he stood. He waved his hands and blinked a few times as his eyes faded back to brown. "I saw the whole thing on the security feeds at the grocery store. One minute that," he said as he pointed to the little monstrosity in the window, "was a normal little girl, running up and down the isles and then," Ivan bared his teeth and held up his hands as if to grab me. "Rawr!"

"Did you see the change?"

"No, she was turned around, standing completely still before she turned and jumped on her mom." Ivan made a face when he saw the little monster hammering on the window. "When Mr. Higgins came over to help, she pushed her mother away and jumped on him. I don't have anything to compare it to on the web. But if I had access to the Other web—"

"No." I was firm with that decision. He and I had had this discussion before and I didn't want him getting close to what could pass as the cyber connections of the Demon Realms. If their magic could change a Witch's nature, then I sure as shit didn't want it messing with my Ivan.

I relinquished my own feed into the wards. The glass lit up with green, blue, yellow and red floating symbols of magic and seals of sorcery. The shell covered the entire store, even down to the basement.

:It's gonna get in! Don't let it in!:

The voice in my head was shrill and full of terror. It wasn't *my* voice, like my inner voice, but the voice of the former Queen of the Unseelie Sidhe, Medbh, whose head now lived in a safe in my basement. Kyle and Ivan could hear her as well, when she wanted them to, but she always wanted me to hear her.

And I'd never heard that kind of fear in her tone. So hearing her beg with what sounded like real terror was a bit disconcerting.

:Do you know what that is?: I asked her, using the same mind thinking at her as she used with me.

No answer. Of course. A Faerie, whether whole or just a head, had two choices when asked a direct question. Tell the truth, or hold its tongue. This one liked biting its tongue. A lot.

"Sam?"

I glanced at Ivan. "Just a sec." I held out both hands this time and summoned my *dex*. Sizable pentagrams flew into position between the monster and myself. Some grew to fill in from ceiling to floor and some shrunk. Once they were in position, they reminded me of the Prague Astronomical Clock before they started spinning in different directions.

The fact the spell didn't come up fast with a definition worried me.

"Damn! Sam look out!"

I lost control of the *dex* when I refocused on the girl outside. She held a cinder block above her head and came charging at the window. At the last second, she threw the block hard against the glass.

It cracked the surface and sent a massive spider web of threads out in every direction—but the glass didn't break. Ha! Lucky I'd paid for the upgrade on bulletproofing!

"That's not going to hold if she does it again."

I heard the sirens seconds before two black and whites screeched to a halt outside the shop in the middle of Bourbon Street. Great. Me and the New Orleans Police Department did not get along. At *all*. They thought I was a huckster and a grifter and I was cheating people out of their money, just like every other two-bit hustler and voodoo priestess in New Orleans.

That, and I'd had a few run-ins with a local detective who also didn't get along with the organization he worked for. We had that in common. I sure as shit hoped *he* didn't come driving up—

Too late, I heard the chest-caving rumble of his '64 Mustang. I looked out the far window to see it pull up behind the squad cars. Detective Crwys Holliard and Detective Levi Tulose charged out of the vintage Mustang and sprinted toward my shop.

Crwys was a bit of a rogue, bad-boy detective. He played fast and loose with department rules and he had a pretty high closed-case rate. He was medium height with a look that Kyle called edgy, with a half-shaved head, piercings similar to Ivan's, and tattoos. He was also sexy as 'effing hell. His eyes were his killer feature…before he took his shirt off. They were a mixture of red and amber and lined with dark, long black lashes.

Eight months ago Crwys and I started a thing, which became a week long marathon of sex and nothing else. It was too easy for me to get lost inside of him, and I don't mean that figuratively. He had raw power and my magical nature was addicted to him. On several occasions, my own magic fed from his.

But Crwys wasn't human. The truth was, I didn't know *what* he was, but my *dex* did say he was Other, which should make him off limits. I lived my life to banish those who invaded our world and harmed people. But Crwys was a cop and never harmed a human if he could help it. He'd proven he was as dedicated to defending innocents as I was.

This one thing gave him a pass with me. No banishing. For now.

His partner on the other hand…

Levi was more of a lady's man. He was handsome, in a sexy Michael Ealy way, wore suits, liked to follow the rules, and always wore shades in the daytime. The two detectives worked nights, so seeing them in the day like this was a bit odd.

Levi was allergic to daylight in certain quantities because he was a Vampire, though his kind preferred to call themselves Revenants. Revenants weren't the gory, overblown sparkly things you see in movies. These were demon-possessed humans. Demon-possessed blood sucking monsters. Creatures from the Demon Realms.

Yeah…he was one of those same creatures I'd dedicated my life to banishing back to their own realm.

Levi got a pass because he worked with Crwys. But if he ever fucked up—his ass was going down.

When Crwys saw the kid, he stopped and I found myself more interested in his reaction than taking stock of the fact the six-year-old was picking the cinder block back up again, hefting it around as if it weighed nothing when in truth it probably weighed more than she did.

The detective looked surprised, but I didn't think it was because of the cinder block.

"Crwys looks confused."

"Yeah. I noticed. And Medbh's screaming her freak'n head off. Whatever this thing is, it's got her scared and him confused."

Ivan put a hand on my shoulder. "I suggest we move back. The cops are pointing guns at the girl. I think the first strike took out that bulletproofing?"

Oh. Good point. I turned, called for Grey and the two of us followed Ivan to the back of the shop and behind the counter. And as every good Cyber Witch was prone to do, Ivan immediately grabbed his computer and set it on the floor behind the counter with us.

Smart boy. Didn't want to lose that. I doubted insurance was going to pay for the damage that little monster had already done, not with what they had to pay six months ago when a Dijin blew out the entire front of the store with a semi.

Yeah. It'd been a rough year.

"Put the block down and turn around, slowly."

Someone with a bullhorn gave the little monster orders. Cute. I doubted they'd noticed the kid was covered in her mother's blood, the eyes or the teeth yet. I hoped none of them were fans of *The Exorcist*, 'cause their childhood nightmares were about to take physical form.

The little monster threw the cinder block again and this time it crashed through the glass and into the bookshelf just past the window. Ivan and I ducked down. I was damn happy he'd suggested we move. Grey licked my face and I hugged her.

The first attempt the monster made at crossing the ward pulled every fine-tuned muscle in my back and spine. It wasn't just trying to break through the ward; it was trying to *annihilate* it, and its maker, on the way in!

I writhed on the floor from the pull on my power. My jaws locked tight as I forced myself not to scream. It felt like one point twenty-one gigawatts of electricity were shooting through my body. I couldn't breathe. I couldn't move. My nails dug half moons into the palms of my hands. I was about to swallow my tongue!

Grey whined and growled but didn't move away from me.

Ivan put his hands on my shoulders and looked helpless. His magic was so foreign to mine, so completely mismatched. He had no way of stopping the link between me and the wards—

And then it was gone. The connection just...snapped.

I sucked in air, gasped for it and marveled at how wonderful it was as it filled my lungs. I grabbed Ivan's forearms just as Grey jumped over me and ran back out into the main part of the shop. I tried to yell for her but I couldn't get enough air in my lungs in time.

Ivan helped me stand so I could see where Grey went. The little monster was still trying to get through the wards and barrier but as soon as Grey bounded up to her, stopping inches from the hole in the glass, the little monster stopped. Its red eyes widened and it hissed at Grey. Grey gave a growl that meant business and snapped at the little fucker.

The monster turned as if to run away and faced one of the NOPD as he stepped from around the door of his squad car. "Come on little girl...it's okay. Don't be frightened of the...dog?"

"Melendez!" Crwys called out as he moved to the back of the officer's car to the left. "Don't get near her."

"She's just a little girl."

"Who killed a grown man and, from what I heard, nearly killed her mother," he pointed to the monster that was now looking at Crwys. "Does she look normal to you? Look at the blood, Melendez. Look at her *teeth*! Step *back*!"

The little monster looked at Crwys and jumped at the officer. It looked like a hopping spider from where I stood with Ivan's support. The thing latched onto his front and bit his face, over and over and over as he fell to the ground. But when Crwys dove to grab her, she let go and ran back to the window, covered in a new coating of blood.

"What the fuck *is* that thing?" Ivan said in a soft voice that vibrated his chest against my cheek.

"I have no damn idea," I muttered. It still seemed familiar to me, but I couldn't put a finger on the memory. Whatever it was, I wasn't sure how to fight it. And I was in no condition to summon any kind of Elemental anything at that moment; much less conjure a banishing pentagram to send it back to wherever it came from.

Grey lunged at that second, a blur of gray and white fur. She tackled the little monster from behind and slammed her to the ground. The thing hissed and kicked as the great wolf bit it on the back of the neck.

Crwys ran forward as others went to the downed and bleeding officer. The detective tentatively reached down, keeping an eye on Grey, and put his hand on the child's back. I'd seen his power before and I knew in that instant what he intended to do. He unleashed that terrible heat of a million suns as it fed through his touch and burned the little monster from the inside out. Within seconds it was ash and no one except me, Ivan and Grey had seen him do it.

This was why I'd broken it off with Crwys Holliard. Whatever he was, it was dangerous.

And I was freak'n terrified of it.

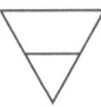

THREE

Robin Tremere pulled up a half hour after the event. I was in the back of my store with an EMT, sucking air from a mask with Crwys by my side. The detective hadn't moved fifty feet away from me since the ambulance, the morgue machine and Crwys's captain arrived on the scene. And I was aware of exactly where he was every second he was within a hundred mile radius of me.

My spent and bruised magic wanted him. My physical self?

I'll check in with you later on that.

Captain Mildred Prescott was not a happy camper. There was a dead grocer, a dead cop, a lot of blood, a broken magic shop and no assailant. And who owned the wolf?

I motioned for Grey to come to me just as I spotted Robin arguing with one of the police officers assigned to guard the perimeter. Crwys noticed and marched up to the officer. They talked and Robin was allowed to come to me. Grey greeted him with her usual indifference as he scratched her neck. The EMT stepped out of the way as my man wrapped his arms around me and held me close. He was warm and non-threatening. He smelled of Halston and was so very, very sanely human.

When he pulled away from me he didn't let go. He kept his hands on my forearms as he looked at me with expressive, red-rimmed eyes. He was the most beautiful man I'd ever known, with short blond hair, soft brown eyes and perfect, perfect lips. He put a hand to my face and brushed hair from my eyes. "Please tell me you're all right. That you're not shot," he glanced behind him at Crwys, who was still too damn close. "Or worse?"

"No. I'm not shot. I'll be fine."

Robin lowered his voice. "Is this about the magic stuff?"

I gave him a weak laugh. Not *at* him, but for him. *With* him. He couldn't see the things Ivan, Kyle and I could. But what caught my heart and kept it was the fact he tried so very, very hard. I pulled the oxygen mask aside and pulled Robin's face to mine so I could kiss him. And because Crwys was right there, I made the kiss last as long as I could.

Of course, I heard the clearing of someone's throat. I disengaged from my boyfriend to see Captain Prescott standing where Crwys had been seconds before. "Miss Hawthorne?"

"Yes ma'am?"

"A word?" she looked at Robin. "Alone?"

Robin put his hand to my cheek. "I'm going to find Kyle and see if he's okay."

"Yeah…might wanna give him a kiss to make him feel better."

"I thought he had a new boyfriend."

I shook my head. "Didn't pass the twenty-four hour mark."

He laughed, nodded to the captain and moved away.

I coughed, grabbed the mask and sucked in more clean oxygen. Not because I had smoke in my lungs, but because I could not get that smell out of my nose and the pure oxygen helped. My chest and every muscle group on every part of my body ached, but I figured it was something a good long, hot bath could cure.

"Well," the captain said as she leaned against the shop's counter. "I see we meet again."

Prescott had been here when the semi took out the front half of the store a few months back. "Yes, ma'am. But I can assure you, I have no relation to or knowledge of the little girl who attacked Mr. Higgins, and the police officer."

"But you saw her. You saw a little girl."

"Yes, ma'am."

"Everyone swears she was real, but all I got is a pile of ash. You see my problem, Miss Hawthorne? But what I do have is a wolf."

"Grey's not a wolf."

"Maybe not, but everyone did see her attack this mysterious little girl."

I did not like where this was going. "My dog attacked the little girl and no one else, ma'am. She did not attack your officer, and she did not attack Mr. Higgins. She was in the shop with me the whole time."

"Simmer down," she held out her hand. "I'm just giving you what you might get from a DA or someone worse up the chain. So be prepared to defend that great beast of yours." Prescott looked around the scene. "You haven't heard anything? Any reports about more kids attacking their parents?"

I blinked at her and ducked my head back. "No. There are more of them? Captain, this kid looked like she was six, maybe seven years old."

"Yes. And she allegedly threw a cinder block at your window." Prescott fixed me with her liquid brown eyes. "A *cinder block*. A six-year-old. Do you see my issue with this?"

I nodded. She has a lot of issues. It was her favorite word.

"Mr. Higgins and Officer Melendez are being transported to the morgue. The mother is on her way to Tulane University Medical Center. And your shop," she turned and looked at the smashed glass. "I suggest you get that boarded up before it gets dark." With that she walked away.

I thanked the EMT, dreaded the bill I knew was coming, and watched him pick his way through the glass to his truck. The officers were slowly driving away. Soon the only cars left on the road were the red Mustang and Robin's Lexus.

Robin helped Kyle and Ivan clean up. Ivan pulled the old boards from the back, the ones we'd used to board up the front of the building after someone tossed a brick through the window after we opened. Crwys stepped outside, put his hand on the remaining glass and within seconds it turned to sand and piled on the floor at his feet.

"Lord and Lady!" I hissed as I stepped through the open door and stood the sidewalk. He'd brought a broom out and was sweeping the glass and sand into a pile. "You can't just do magic like that!"

"No one noticed. It's just us. And you forget what I taught you. Humans can't really see what we're doing while we're in certain parts of the city." Once he had the debris swept aside he motioned for Ivan to set the first board in place. Crwys held it as Ivan and Robin hammered it into position.

I hated the dual feeling I had around Crwys. The deep desire to touch him and the uncomfortable wish to banish him. But he wouldn't tell me what he was. He wouldn't trust me even that much. His need for secrecy annoyed me. I didn't like secrets. They always came back to bite us in the ass, and one day, Crwys's ass was going to get chomped.

That's why I was with Robin now. He didn't have any secrets to keep from me.

Crwys spoke in a low voice. "That was a Changeling."

I froze. That's it! That's why it seemed so familiar. I'd faced one before and watched as it was burned to death, just as Crwys had done. Changelings were left by the Sidhe when they took human children into *Alfheim*. But they didn't leave the Changelings to take a stolen child's place. Changelings were there to get rid of the evidence left behind. Usually the entire family.

I soured on the whole fairy tale angle. Who knew the Grimm brothers got it wrong?

He pointed at me as he let go of the board and it stayed in place. Robin and Kyle had it half tacked up. "Your face tells me you know what that is. I haven't seen a Changeling in decades. In fact, it's been ages since I've even heard of one showing up. Then about a year ago there was one up in Seattle. No one thought it was a Changeling but me. Then nothing. And now, in the span of three days and eleven deaths, this is the sixth Changeling Levi and I have seen."

Lord and Lady! "Six Changelings in three days? What the hell? Did a Faerie Queen suddenly decide she wanted a Viking horde of kids? I mean, if you exchange it for the real thing—then where are the real children?"

Crwys nodded to the store. "We could always ask."

He meant heading down into the bowels of the shop and asking Medbh. Very few knew she was down there.

I watched Kyle, Robin and Ivan finish boarding up the window and didn't answer. Crwys finally walked into the back of the shop. As for Levi, the Revenant, I assumed he was inside as well, keeping out of the sun.

After the glass and sand were removed and safely inside rubber trash bins, I stepped back in. Kyle had turned his attention to picking up what was left of the bookshelf the cinder block had taken out. I paused to help him, and when he didn't speak, I touched his arm. "You okay?"

When he looked at me I saw he wasn't. His eyes looked sunken, and dark half moons hung under them. His face looked gaunt and he was pale. When I'd been writhing on the floor as the Changeling tried to enter, I knew Kyle had suffered a similar trauma.

I had felt the assault on a physical level, which was how my magic worked because I powered it with my own energy. My soul, my katra, my essence. Kyle would have felt it on a mental level because a Hedge Witch like himself, used their mind and imagination to summon, hold and direct magic. Yeah, they needed the ritual and symbology, the physical trappings and essence of herbs to *energize* the magic, but the control came from their minds. He probably had one hell of a headache.

"Go home, Kyle. Get some rest."

"No. I can't do that. Not after what I felt and saw."

"Crwys says it was a Changeling," I watched Kyle's expression as he continued picking things up and piling them into his arms. "Like in the fairy tales."

"I take it a Changeling isn't what I think it is."

"No. He wants to talk to Medbh."

Kyle turned a pained and angry gaze toward me. "I think that's a fucking great idea." He stood and took his handful of books into the back.

When I pushed up on my thighs to stand, Robin moved beside me and took me into his arms. The top of my head tucked perfectly under his chin. It felt so good when he held me. My magic stayed in check, there was no overwhelming longing to throw him down on the floor and summon the two-backed beast like I had with Crwys, though Robin and I had a nice rhythm going. I didn't want him to leave. But I sensed something was up when he pulled back and he kissed my nose. "You're not staying?"

"I have to get to my sister's, remember? Drop off my key?"

Crap! Right. We were supposed to go together. His sister Rose was making dinner and I'd been looking forward to seeing the kids. Robin's sister was three years younger than him, a single mom with two beautiful daughters. One of them had a spark about her and I sensed the God Mother's blood in her instantly. This was something I hadn't shared with Robin or Rose. A child's choice to follow the Path was their own. And if her magic never matured enough to use, then the better it would be for her to lead and enjoy a normal life.

"Hey, don't worry," he said as he moved his thumb over my lower lip. "I'll tell her what happened. Well, I'll tell her the highlights, about a killer loose in the neighborhood. She's probably already heard about Higgins so I'll make the excuse that you need to stay here."

This was the truth, just not for the reasons I was sure he'd tell Rose. I kissed his thumb and then pulled him in close for another passionate kiss on his full and desirable lips. He hugged me again and whispered in my ear. "If you can, come to my house. I'd feel better if you were with me tonight and not here."

"Okay," was all I said. I had his spare key, which was why he was dropping off a new one to his sister. "When I'm done, I'll be over. Oh, after I grab an overnight bag."

"You know you can just leave things with me."

Yeah, I knew it. But we'd only seen each other six months, and I wanted to take it slow. Especially after the *Flame On* relationship with Crwys and then that disastrous two-night rebounder with a guy I knew from high school. I had no idea the asshole was a woman beater. I still remember the first and only time he tried to hit me and found himself looking down the barrel of one of my Smith & Wessons. I had two of them, each appropriately named. Lord for the right hand, and Lady for the left. Their names were engraved in Gaelic on their sides along with the appropriate symbols for Earth, Air, Water and Fire.

No, they didn't shoot magic, but *infused* with magic, they never missed.

He said goodbye to Kyle and Ivan, waved at Crwys and I walked him out to his car. After watching him drive away, I turned back to the shop, only to have Crwys inches from my face.

"Crap on a dragon's balls, don't do that!" I shouted at him as I put my hand on my chest and coaxed my heart out of my throat.

But Crwys wasn't deterred in the least. "I don't like him. And I still don't know why you say that."

"Say what?"

"Crap on a dragon's balls? Why not just plain crap like everyone else."

"Because I'm not everyone else. Why? You partial to dragons?"

"I'm partial to defending creatures that have no voice for themselves."

I rolled my eyes at him. "As for Robin, you don't like anybody. I think it's because of what you are." I moved past him and headed back to the front door.

"But you don't even know what I am," he said as he followed behind me.

"Because you won't tell me."

"Not till you tell me about your mother."

I stopped right in front of the door and spun around. This time he had to back pedal so as not to run into me. I had my hands balled into fists and I was very much aware they were glowing with the soft blue witch light of my power. "Why are you so damn curious about my mother? You just can't let it go."

Crwys noticed my fists, but if they worried him, he didn't show it. "Just curious why you never mention her, or never talk about her."

"Fuck. Off." I pushed the Air Element between us and shoved him back a few feet. He stayed upright, another testament to the fact he wasn't human. A normal person would have flown ass over end across the road into the opposite building.

I reigned in my anger, shook off the ache in my hands and headed to the back. "Kyle, Ivan, we're having a meeting with the head."

FOUR

When I say a meeting with the head—that's exactly what I mean.

My reason for having the head of the former Unseelie Queen in my basement was a long and complicated story. She was the reason I knew about Changelings, since one had been sent into this world to kill someone I knew. It surprised me that I didn't recognize what that little girl was outside the shop and reminded myself to update my *dex* database.

Given what was in my basement, one would think a severed head would rot and feed maggots and just become generally nasty. But the moment it passed from the land of Faerie, *Alfheim*, to this world, it became a creepy, ceramic doll head.

And worse…it talked. As far as I could figure out, the spirit of Medbh was still inside. Not knowing what else to do with it, I locked it in the basement under a thick layering of wards and popped it out now and then to ask it a question. Sometimes she answered, sometimes she didn't. Just like she didn't say anything when I asked her if she knew what the little girl was. I figured, when she didn't want to answer, it was because the answer went against Faerie secrets, or queen secrets, or she was just PMSing.

Her stubbornness at not answering sometimes put Crwys in a bad mood, and he had on more than one occasion thrown the ugly-assed thing to the ground. The first time that happened I was sort of relieved. I thought I'd be done with Faerie.

Nope.

Two days later her voice was back and her head had reformed, though the left eye was now messed up where a crack bisected it and some of the ceramic had chipped away. Now it was a *cracked*, creepy ceramic doll head. And if the head ever met the body…well…

Bad things, baby.

The basement was laid out in three rooms. The first room housed the hot water heater as well as the breaker box for the shop. I kept boxes of supplies down there in water safe tubs, just in case. Through a door to the right was another longer, narrower room with metal shelves. This was where I stored the creepier things I found, like shrunken heads and cursed amulets. They were stored in boxes and well labeled. Not many of them. Maybe three?

At the far end was the third room. It measured five by five with only one way in. The door into the room locked from the outside and Kyle had wondered if the church that'd occupied the shop a decade ago had used this room for exorcisms.

I didn't believe in things like that. Once a demon was inside of a person, their only salvation was death.

Speaking of demons and possession, Levi, who stayed out of the way and found a nice dark corner to stay in after the Changeling incident, followed us into the basement. Ivan had set up bar stools in the largest room with the creepy stuff and a table in the center.

Everyone but Kyle and I picked out a stool as we opened the small room, and then opened the iron safe inside of it. The head was shrouded in a burlap peanut bag. No special reason, other than Medbh hated it.

:About time you asked for my advice again, girl. It gets lonely and dark shut up in that old safe.:

Sometimes customers heard Medbh's voice. I think she did that on purpose just to remind me she was there. Her singing and off color remarks gave my shop the reputation of being haunted. I didn't mind. The disembodied voice brought in business.

I was gonna need more business once I called the insurance.

I never directly touched the head. Not because I was afraid of it or thought the old girl could contaminate me. It was just too creepy to touch. Like putting my hand on a tarantula.

Just wasn't going to happen.

Grey sat beside my stool, saving it so no one else would sit there. Levi and Crwys stood because they were interlopers.

:Oh, it's so nice to see everyone.: Medbh's voice shifted a lot. Sometimes she sounded like Aunt B from *Mayberry R.F.D.*, and sometimes she sounded like one of the girls from the movie, *Mean Girls*. It just depended on her mood. Today she sounded like Aunt B. *:And you, Crwys, doing such a nice job getting rid of that Changeling.:* I think she mimicked that voice because she could hear my television upstairs. I didn't have cable and I was guilty of falling asleep on the couch with the TV on. I woke up many a morning to the sound of Andy Griffith and Don Knots.

Crwys glanced at me and I knew it was a look of *told you it was a Changeling*, since no one had actually asked her a question yet.

"Thank you, Medbh," Crwys said as he crossed his arms over his chest. "But what we need to know—and if you don't answer my question I'll break your little head again—is why it's here in the first place. Was she one of yours?"

Medbh didn't answer at first, but the head did rock and shift where it sat on the table until it faced Crwys. To me, *that* was creepier than the thing actually talking. I didn't like things that weren't supposed to move. And doll heads were on the top of the list. *:There is no need to resort to violence. That vagabond was not one of mine. I haven't had a Changeling in the game since…:* and it rocked a bit to face me. *:Since I made the one that killed the new queen's mother.:*

Yep. You heard that right. The new Unseelie Queen was one of Medbh's former victims.

Levi held up a hand. "Can someone fill me in on this new queen? What the hell is she talking about?"

I didn't feel like rehashing shit from the past, but Levi needed to be brought up to speed. Luckily Crwys stepped in and filled that roll. Sort of. He did a Crwys-style recap. "This annoying head belongs to the previous Obsidian Queen of the Sidhe, the Unseelie Queen. She's a head because a Witch she turned into one of her wolves bit her head *off*. The last Changeling Medbh here remembers making is the one she left to take the place of *that* Witch," he glanced at his partner. "That make sense?"

"Sure, sure."

But I knew Levi wasn't any more informed than he was before.

And since it was a direct question answered and nothing dire happened to the head, we could all assume she was being truthful. Which meant Medbh wasn't making the Changelings attacking randomly in the city.

"Then who made the six that have been killing people? Are they all in this area?" I glanced at Crwys.

He gave me a nod.

Medbh's head shifted again, as if facing everyone. I had to wonder if she could really see, or if it was that blind sensing thing. :*You'd have to ask the new queen. Only she could answer that.*:

Well, screw that. "Sorry, that's not gonna happen." I'd made a deal with the new queen nine months ago and reneged on it, so I was persona non grata when it came to the new Obsidian Queen. No one ever breaks a promise with the Faerie and lives well. Or lives at all. The only thing separating me from Faerie capture, torture and death was the new queen's father, who asked her to pardon me.

And she did.

But I didn't want to take any chances.

"What about the Silver Queen and her Daoine Sidhe? Could she know something?" Crwys asked.

Medbh didn't have shoulders, but the movement her head made looked like a shrug. :*I suppose. But you'll have to make sure the ground is firmly sanctioned between worlds. Tzariene is particularly allergic to this world and she rarely ever takes a body.*:

I knew what Medbh meant by allergic. Those of the Faerie blood couldn't live in our world for very long. Once the sunlight found them, or their feet touched the ground, Faeries turned to ash. Which I considered a plus, given my personal history with them. This was why we kept Medbh's head away from the sun.

As for taking a body, it was possible for some of the Faerie folk to inhabit human bodies just like most of the races of the Demon Worlds.

But the effort was hard on them and human hosts usually went mad while being possessed, which made it even more difficult for the Faerie to escape, or toss them out.

"Tzariene?" Levi said. "Who is that?"

"That's the Silver Queen's name." Crwys rubbed at his chin with his fingers.

I glanced at Kyle and Ivan. They were paying attention but unusually silent. Especially Kyle.

Levi spoke up again. "What does she mean by sanctioned land?"

Ivan spoke up. "Sacred. Purified. Sanctified. Has to be consecrated by magic for a Faerie to stand on it," he looked at Kyle. "Your aunt's land pretty much stays in that condition, doesn't it? That's where you and Sam did that ritual to talk to Brendi."

Brendi was the name of the new Unseelie Queen.

"Yeah but my aunt still hasn't forgiven me for that." Kyle bent forward and rested his elbows on his knees.

"It's not your fault your cousin lied to you when she said you had permission."

"Doesn't matter. It's my fault for not following the permission up the chain of command. Trust me, I got off with a warning. My cousin?" Kyle made a sad face. "I'm not sure where the body's buried."

The bad thing about that was I wasn't so sure he was kidding.

Kyle's aunt, Arden Vervain, was possibly the scariest Witch I knew. Entrepreneur, self-made billionaire, with a no-nonsense southern charm that would straighten General Lee's beard.

God Mother's Gifts weren't always understandable. No one knew why Witches like myself possessed four Gifts with the possibility of attaining a fifth, when some only held one or two. Our Magical Parliament couldn't explain it. The only thing they did through the centuries was create and enforce what I thought was an outdated model that put single Gift users at the bottom of the food chain, and higher numbered users at the top.

The fact I had four Gifts with potential for another made me a candidate for leader or Elder, which I perfunctorily refused and used that stupidity as a reason to disassociate myself from that branch of magical government. This didn't endear me to the Parliament or their brute squad, also know as the Clerics of Peace.

Or magical mayhem squad, as I referred to them.

Groups like the New Orleans Eldership were elected by Gift rank. The leadership's power was determined by the High Witch of each state, and that position was held in secret. No one knew which of the nine Witches on each governing council was the High Witch. This rule dated back to the Trials, when Witches used magical names in order to hide their true identities from the Witch Finders. As crazy as that sounded—Witch Finders still exist. Humans who possess just enough of the Gift to give them sight but not attainable magic, made them aware of magic so they can see it, and sense it, often use this Gift to find Witches, and destroy them.

Rules were set by the Parliament and policed by the Clerics, all ranking at no less than three Gifts. We had three Cleric Hives for Louisiana and Mississippi, one member of which I knew intimately, because she'd raised me from the time I was eight. My guardian and local Cleric, Inamorata Devonshire.

Arden Vervain possessed three Gifts. Elemental Gifts were regarded the highest. She had Water and Earth, and her third magic was called a Dianic Gift. She had the power of a Seer. This combination assured her of being a member of a Council anywhere she went.

Her nephew Kyle, if left to be ranked and judged in that society, would be at the bottom rung because his Gifts weren't seen as natural. Truth was Kyle could manipulate any Gift the God Mother made with his use of ritual and spell. I'd seen him gather all four of the Elements together in a single spell to heal. I'd seen him burn roots to see into the future, or pulverize and steep a tea to "hear" another's thoughts.

The fact Arden couldn't see the wonder in Kyle's Hedge abilities stymied me to no end. So she kept him at a distance and, I think, "tolerated" the fact that I, an Elemental Witch, encouraged him to practice his magic.

Given these rules—can you imagine how Ivan fit into this hegemony?

I met Arden only once, and unfortunately exposed my own

natural abilities, which she wanted to add to her coven. It's the largest grouping of Witches in the Southeast, and the most powerful. Little got by Arden's network of informants. I was pretty sure she already knew about the Changelings and the murders.

"If you plan on contacting that nut case, you'll excuse me if I bow out of that little meet and greet," Crwys said as he lowered his hands. "I'll do a bit of investigating on my own."

"Like what?" I asked him.

"Like that smell. I know you know what I mean," he nodded to me and then he looked at Ivan. "And you smelled it as well."

"What was it?" Ivan asked.

"Arcane," Crwys shifted his gaze to the little head. "Care to enlighten us on that, Medbh?"

:What's to enlighten? Arcane is the magic of the Demon Worlds, as Samantha likes to call them. I myself am animated in this head through Arcane. My world, all the worlds except this one, exist with Arcane Magic,: she laughed. *:If I were reunited with my body, you would all be personally acquainted with what Arcane Magic can do.:*

I stood and moved in close. As I knelt down to stare into those dead and damaged ceramic eyes, Grey came up beside me and gave the ugly little thing a low growl. "Let's get one thing straight. I can take a hammer and pulverize you into dust any time I want. Let's see how well your great and powerful Arcane Magic can reform this little vessel after that. Or I can take you into the parking lot and drink a mint julep while I watch the sun do the dirty work. Either way, I own your bitchy ass. So another threat like that? And I will do one of the two. Got it?"

Medbh didn't answer for a few seconds, and then. *:I got it. Geez… you really need to lighten up.:*

"Good. So let's recap? You didn't create the Changelings murdering people these past couple of days?"

:No.:

"And you don't know if there are more?"

:No.:

"But you do agree whatever is doing this is using Faerie shenanigans."

When Medbh hesitated we all paid attention. Grey stood up on her back legs and put her paws on the table. She opened her jaw and picked up the head in her mouth before she sat back and held it precariously over the concrete floor.

:AAEEEIIII! Get this monster away from me! Put me down!:

"Answer the question."

:Then make it a question.:

"Do you believe whatever is creating these Changelings or controlling them is using Faerie Magic?"

She hesitated again. *:Yes.:*

I glanced over at Crwys. His reddish amber eyes were narrowed and he gave me an almost imperceptible nod. I looked back at Medbh. "Do you believe it is a Faerie doing it?"

:No. But not because I'm psychic. We're not this stupid. Sending Changelings out like that in broad daylight is a sure attention grabber. Especially in a place as thickly populated as this. What's the payoff? Why do it? The only reason I can come up with is that someone is trying to grab attention. But I don't know if that's everyone's attention, or someone in particular.:

I straightened up. Fair enough. "All right. Time for you to go back in the box." I grabbed the peanut bag and carefully pried Medbh's head from Grey's jaws with it. I gave her a wink and a smile and she opened her mouth with her tongue hanging out. It was good enough of a smile for me.

:Don't leave me alone.:

"You won't be alone. I'll be here," Ivan stood up from his stool. "I don't think my tagging along to Miss Vervain's is a good idea. I don't want her knowing a damn thing about me."

I didn't want her knowing either.

I shoved the now quiet Medbh back into her safe, reset the wards and followed everyone back up the steps. We gathered in the back break room kitchen. Ivan started coffee. Kyle pulled out his phone and headed out the back dock door, presumably to call his aunt.

I followed Crwys and Levi through the shop to the front door. Levi stepped outside to light a cigarette. Crwys stopped at the door and turned to me. "You and Robin…everything's all right?"

I knitted my eyebrows together at him. "What the hell do you care? You said you didn't like him."

"But you do."

"So?"

"What you like is important to me."

"Crwys," I said as I took a step back and he took a step toward me. "*This* isn't going to happen."

"What? You and Robin? That's too bad."

I continued backing up until I hit a shelf of books. I stuck my finger out and stopped him from getting too close. But he was still blocking my view of everything. "Crwys. No."

"It's not over, Sam. It can't be. I don't understand why you keep pushing me away."

"The fact that I lost twelve days of my life in bed with you." I pushed him back again with another poke of my finger against his hard chest. "You're not healthy for me, Crwys. And our magic…"

"Yes."

I had to move to the side to get out of his direct line of fire. Damn. Being that close to the boy made all parts south come to attention. I held out my hands as I backed up. "I'm with Robin. Let's just work with that."

Crwys took in a deep breath, and released an even longer, deeper sigh. "Okay. I did promise to give you space." As he turned to the door he said, "Levi and I are gonna head to the hospital. Need to talk to that mother before it's too late."

"Too late for what?"

His brows rose up high on his forehead as he looked back at me. "Changelings are killing machines, Sam. They don't leave prey unscathed. They excrete poison in their bite. So anyone bitten by a Changeling is going to die. That woman doesn't have long to live."

I stood in the broken shop for several minutes after he left, letting my libido come to a full stop before getting off the ride. I thought about how close Ivan and I had come to that thing breaking through those wards, and thanked whatever power had stopped it from happening.

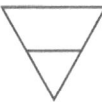

FIVE

My brain hurt and I was achy from making magic. I preferred preparation when I did things like that. Spell casting on the fly wasn't always the best way to cast. I likened it to eating healthy or eating fast food. Fast was easier, but the side effects were bad for the body.

I shuffled past the counter to the door in the center that led to the break room.

When I leased the store, I partitioned off the inside in a less than traditional design. There was less retail area than storage and rear space. I had a small kitchen installed in the break room area and recently came into the possession of a twelve foot long oak table King Arthur would have been proud of.

I gave everyone a place to eat their lunch, exchange their gossip, and if the weather was just too unpleasant, a place to draw down the moon. I lived in the apartment above the shop, which seemed a long-standing tradition in New Orleans. I had the choice of renting the space out to make more money, or making it mine.

Given the hard work I put into making the store a success that at least paid for the basic necessities, I figured staying close to my investment was a better idea. Not to mention rental rates in New Orleans were ridiculously expensive, unless I found a house in Iberia. And that was just too far of a drive to work for me.

Grey stuck her nose between my legs and I lowered my arms to give her some good, easy scratches behind her ears. "It's all right girl. We'll figure out what's going on."

"Sam, you want some tea?" Ivan said from the stove.

It was just me and my guys again. And a very empty and wounded store. Even Medbh was quiet.

I walked further into the kitchen, suddenly thinking back to what had severed the connection between the Changeling and our wards. I replayed the event in my head and the only conclusion I came up with was a bit on the unbelievable side. "Ivan…when the little monster was trying to get through the ward, I was being tortured."

"Yeah," he said as he glanced over at me. He poured water from the electric kettle into two mugs with tea bags. English breakfast. My favorite.

"And then it was gone. It just broke," I narrowed my eyes at him. "Did you do that?"

He stared at the cups as he pulled the tea bags up and then dunked them back in, over and over again. "I didn't hurt you, did I?"

"No. In fact I think I would have been in worse shape if you hadn't of. But…*how* did you do it? I thought your Cyber Magic didn't mesh with…well regular magic." I hated to call my magic regular because it made his sound like it was irregular.

Truth was, we just didn't know enough about it. Learning to use it for Ivan was a lot like discovery through trap doors.

"It doesn't, most of the time. I mean I can't really see what it is you do. I can feel it. It raises the hairs on my arms. But where you can see parts of what I see, your magic is a complete mystery to me." He stopped dunking the tea and turned to face me. I was struck again by the exotic beauty of his features. His father's dark, Eurasian eyes accented by his mother's Spanish nose and jaw line were perfectly framed by that mane of thick black hair he kept cut close to his face. "When you started contorting—and you were seriously contorting, Sam—I freaked out. My magic kicked in and reached out in all directions because I was desperate to help you. And then I saw it. Ugly little red wiggling worms in rows as they wrapped around you. They were encased in what looked like blue white tubes.

"I looked over the counter and I saw millions of those nasty red worms flying out from that Changeling and it reminded me of communication hubs. Packets of information coming in and going out. I thought of the data-stream on the web and the different colors certain communications have for me. Blue and white are always personal, like email and texting a loved one. Green is always there for financial transactions. Yellow comes in as the communication of industry. Company missives. But then there are the ones that are red or orange, and they've always shown me where the bad creators are. The hackers. The spoofers. The ones that mean harm. I interpreted all those worms as harm and I just…" he held out his hands. "I reached out and cut the communication."

What struck me at that moment was that I understood him. I'd always seen things as colors myself, but they were the colors of Elements. Red, blue, green and yellow. Different days always had color for me, as did numbers and emotions.

Ivan had just told me, in so many words, that he'd actually *seen* Arcane Magic. Even I couldn't *see* Arcane. I could smell it. I could sense it. But not *see* it.

I put a hand on his arm. "Ivan…I think you just leveled up, so to speak. You were seeing Arcane and you actually affected it. You stopped its use."

Now his eyes matched the size of mine. "I was? I did?"

The back door opened and Kyle came back in. He looked… abused.

"Uh oh. Witch Queen didn't play nice?" I asked, and then regretted it. Damn outside voice.

He shook his head. "It's all good. Apparently my aunt already knows about what's happened. She wants to meet with us," he looked at Ivan. "Even you."

"No." I shook my head. "I don't think Ivan should go. Remember what happened last time?"

Last time was a reference to my first meeting with Arden. Ivan had come with me to help exorcise a spectre out of a patron's basement. Ivan had tapped into the house's electrical system, making sure the spectral anomalies in the basement weren't being caused by magnetic fields. Arden burst in, having heard I was at the house of one of her

Society buddies, and boasted how she was quite capable of getting rid of the problem herself.

Arden doesn't have the power to banish or exorcise anything. The only reason I could come up with for the reason she did what she did was for theatrical effect.

And boy-howdy, that's what she got. The woman blasted the house with a dose of something toxic—which I later learned was an exorcism spell she found in a book of eighteenth century poetry—and managed to fry every electrical outlet in the house.

The blowback knocked Ivan into a coma for two days.

And the patron? Haven't seen her since.

"She didn't know what she was doing. And besides, she still thinks he's just a Dianic candidate."

I spoke up. "No. She gets me and you and Grey. No Ivan. She's got to earn my trust."

Ivan nodded. "I'll stay here. Lock up."

I checked the clock. Damn. It was already after five. "Yeah I guess we're closed anyway. What time does she want us there?"

"She's at her home in the Garden District," Kyle looked worried. "As soon as we can get there."

I wasn't in the mood to deal with Arden Vervain just yet. I need a little bit of a pick me up. "Kyle, get home and get a shower, or go upstairs if you don't want to go home first. I'll be back in about an hour."

"Where you going?" Ivan called out after me and when I looked back, he had my tea in his hand.

Oops. "Heading over to Ina's. I need a little boost."

SIX

Inamorata Devonshire lived in the north end of the Garden District, not far from Kyle's apartment. I dropped him off first, since he chose to take a shower at his place and promised I'd be back in an hour.

The afternoon moved from crisp October sunshine into a more monochromatic hue as clouds moved in. The weather report on my Jeep's radio said the chance of afternoon showers had moved form zero to forty percent. "We better hope that's for after our visit, Grey, or we're gonna have wet seats."

Grey, seated in the back with her head and shoulders between the driver's seat and the passenger's, nuzzled my right ear and made a small *wuff* of agreement. I had a hard top, but it was stored in the back of the shop where I usually parked the Jeep. I kept a tarp in a locker in the back just in case of sudden rain showers.

Ina's house reminded me of the sister's house in the movie *Candle Magic*. It had the same architecture, the same front porch, the same side porch with the arbor, and the same twisting and wide spaced rooms inside. What it didn't have was the center tower with the lookout on top. Which was fine by me since I was afraid of heights. The house sat back from the road, half hidden among a jungle of trees, plants, shrubs and weeds. An iron gate circled the entire property, but that wasn't what protected the place.

No…that was something else entirely.

Like I said before, Ina was a Cleric. One of the duties that came with this position was the enormous responsibility of warding magic and magic places of business from the eyes of the Cowen, those not Gifted with the God Mother's blessing. To any passing tourist, neighbor or visiting relative, the house never registered on their radar. People passed by the wrought iron gate day and night, but none ever noticed the grand house and its beautiful gardens as they passed.

Ina raised me after my mom was killed, but we didn't live in this house. She moved in and took care of me and my dad at our house in Picayune, Mississippi. I'd always called her Aunt Ina. It wasn't until I was eighteen that she told me she wasn't really my aunt. She and my mom had been best friends, coven-mates, but never blood sisters. That didn't matter to me. Ina was family, regardless of blood.

And she was the only other Witch I knew I could turn to. Ina had taught me all that I knew. It wasn't considered conventional teaching. It wasn't part of a coven and it wasn't out of some pre-approved book like a lot of the Gifted were taught these days. Ina believed in what she called the Old Ways. I'd learned these ways and the *new* ways didn't always play well together.

I parked the Jeep outside the front gate where there was always parking for family. Odd how tourists and others living in the neighborhood never took that particular spot. Grey jumped out as I unlocked the back trunk under the seat and pulled out the tarp. I had it tied on top within minutes. Eh…it wouldn't keep out the backsplash if the rain was hard and fast. But if it kept to a sprinkle, I could at least keep our butts dry when I picked up Kyle.

The front door opened as Grey and I walked up the stone-laid path. Grey ran on ahead and Ina knelt down to greet her. The two became fast friends the moment they met, and sometimes I was a little jealous of their closeness. Usually Grey would always come to me and rest her head in my lap on the couch. But not if Ina was around.

"Merry meet!" Ina called out from her position on the porch with Grey. "Looks like rain." She frowned and stood as she came to the edge of the porch. "Samantha Elizabeth—you didn't have to put the tarp on. Just cover it with a—"

I held up my hand to stop her scolding. "And try and explain why my Jeep isn't wet while the rest along the street are? No thanks."

I came up the steps and took in the smell from the wisteria growing over the trellis. I also caught the scent of magnolia from the trees in the back.

Ina was a few inches taller than me, with snow-white hair always held back in a single silver clip. Most of her wardrobe consisted of loose fitting clothes of cotton and soft knits, layered folds and coordinated colors. Today she wore wide black pants, a dark green wrap top covered by a soft gray cover, one of those with infinite folds in the front. Her jewelry matched with grays and silver and green, except for the silver pentagram hanging from a delicate chain at her neck. This piece of jewelry she never removed.

Grey and I preceded her in and I felt an instant boost of confidence just from the aura of the place. Antique couches, side tables, a coat rack and large mantel fireplace greeted visitors alike, but I followed Grey further into the larger family room. Bean bag chairs, papasans, two overstuffed couches all gathered in a circle facing a large flat screen TV over a smaller fireplace. This is where Ina taught her own brand of magic with her students. The smells of something spicy filled the house and I moved past the family room to the large, spacious kitchen.

"What smells so good?"

Grey joined me and poked her nose under my hand.

"Boiled newt and dragon's wing." Ina stepped in and removed the top from a large pot on the stove. She took a wooden spoon from a stand on the counter and started stirring.

I was used to Ina's oddly colorful jokes about what she and I were. I peered inside and sniffed again. "Stew…is it beef?"

"Yep. Jackson and Earl brought me a half cow about a month ago. So I've been trying different recipes. This has a brisket in it," she grabbed a spoon, skimmed off the top and held it out for me. "You tell me. I've burned my tongue so many times I can't taste anything anymore."

I carefully took the spoon and blew on the broth. I saw small slivers of potato and carrots floating about before I tasted the thick broth. I closed my eyes and savored the taste. I wanted to cook like Ina, but that was just not a talent I found I could master. "Mmm…damn Ina. That is good. Who're you feeding?"

She took the spoon back and set it in the sink. "My Dianic students are coming over tonight. We'll all be doing different things for All Hallows, so we're getting together as a group tonight for a party. I was gonna start decorating…" Ina said as she tilted her head to her shoulder. "But you need to talk to me about something else. First, have you been practicing your Elemental scales?"

"Yes Ina, but—"

"And you've been continuing to combine the four Elements for spell casting and integration?"

"Whenever I can. But Ina—"

"And you've made sure to stay as far away from Arcane Magic as possible?"

I finally just gave up and sighed. "I haven't tried to use it, I haven't read about it and I haven't investigated it." That was only a half-truth. Where Ina thought it best not to know about the things that were bad for us, I thought it best we educate ourselves or rather I educate myself. I had to know what I was up against if I wanted to defeat it and banish it.

Ina arched a brow at me and stopped talking. I never knew if that was a signal that she knew I'd been lying or if she was actually looking into my soul. "Okay. Why are you here?"

"You been watching the news?"

Ina shook her head. "Not today. I've been in here cooking. Got two pies in the oven. An apple and a cherry. I also have water boiling. Why don't you and Grey find a place to get comfortable? I'll bring you both something and we'll talk. I think you have maybe…an hour?"

I grinned at her. "How do you do that?"

"Let's see. Your shoulders are all hunched and bunched, you've got your mother's crease between your eyebrows and Grey already told me."

That was another thing that I wasn't sure about. Ina insisted she and Grey talked to one another. Which was ridiculous. But was it? I ignored it and let Grey lead me into the garden room.

Now *this* room was a room I wanted on my apartment balcony. Pots and pots of herbs and flowers lined the shelves, tables and stools scattered about, as well as the steps as we entered. The smells were out of this world. There were so many I could never pin point a single one. On one side of the room where the plants were sparse was a floor to ceiling case with four shelves from about my waist up, all lined with glass bottles and varied shape containers. In each was a dried herb or something weird I didn't want to try and identify. Below my waist were six drawers, each filled the accoutrements needed to keep a garden this size growing.

Near the shelf was a decent sized table, an antique Ina turned into her work area. On it were scraps of things, from bits of used candles, string, herbs and her white handled knife, the ritual working knife of most Witches.

The jungle of plants surrounded a set of natural wicker furniture. A sofa, two chairs and a coffee table. Ina had covered the coffee table with a piece of wood cut to size and glued down. Woven wicker did not make a flat, even top for use.

I plopped down on the left side of the sofa and Grey jumped on the sofa with me and rested her head in my lap. I stroked her neck and along the top of her head. "Can you really talk to Ina, girl? Or is she as crazy as people say?"

"I'm not crazy," Ina said as she brought a tray out with two cups, a container of natural sweetener, one sugar, a plastic bear of honey, spoons, a plate of chocolate cookies, and a larger bowl full of the stew!

She set the tray down on the coffee table and put the bowl on the floor. Grey slipped off the couch and started lapping up the stew.

"I don't know if that's good for her," I said as I peered over the side and watched. "I mean, you're not supposed to feed animals from the table."

"You feed her Chinese food. So don't go off on me. Besides, Grey likes my stew." Ina arranged herself on one of the chairs and started decorating her tea. "Fix it the way you like and tell me why you're here. I hope it's not about that crazy boy."

The crazy boy Ina referred to was Crwys. The two hadn't officially met yet, so the only opinion she'd formed was from what I told her. I was honest and admitted I couldn't put a finger on what he was, which intrigued her. But I wasn't about to take her up on her invitation to invite him over so she could do a little investigating on her own. "It's not Crwys."

"Then it's about the nice Cowen boy you're seeing?" She took her tea and sat back in her chair.

Thinking the word Cowen in my head was always preferable to saying it out loud. It wasn't my favorite word, but it had its place. I figured it was sort of like *Harry Potter's* Muggles, though Cowen was a much older term. "Robin's fine. It's about something that happened today."

I started at a decent pace as I told her about what happened. But by the time I got to Crwys mentioning the poison in a Changeling's teeth I was talking fast again. I do that when I get excited.

Grey finished her stew, licked her lips and went back through the door. I assumed if Ina hadn't laid out a bowl of water, she was going to find a toilet to drink out of.

I watched as Ina set her tea back down and I picked mine up. It was cold now, but it didn't matter. I downed it all at once and felt the herbs she'd slipped into it working to clear my head and rejuvenate.

Ina was a Hedge Witch, just as Kyle was, but Ina carried three Gifts, two Elemental that developed not long after my mother died. Air and Water.

"Someone is using Faerie Magic to control Changelings."

"That was Medbh's opinion."

"And you're sure it was a direct question?"

"Yes."

"Was Grey there?"

That came out of left field. What was Grey's importance when speaking to Medbh? "Yeah. We were all there. And nothing bad happened. No discoloring, no marks, no agony. None of the stuff you said happens to Faeries who lie."

Ina looked satisfied, though sometimes it was hard to tell with her. "And you're sure about Ivan? This is what he saw? And he just… severed the connection?"

"Yeah. Ina, we're just not sure when it comes to Ivan. So you *cannot* tell anyone about this. I don't want Parliament to know about him yet." In truth, I was afraid if they discovered Ivan's type of magic, they would request an audience with him, and that would mean a trip to Oregon. Witches summoned to an audience with Parliament rarely returned with little or no explanation.

"Oh hell, Sam. I don't tell anyone anything. Especially not that little group of old biddies. But I have spoken to your dad. You should really drive over to Picayune and visit him from time to time."

I bristled at the thought. I loved my dad. I really did. But I was not a fan of his new wife. Which was why I had followed Ina out of Mississippi. "Yeah, maybe for Yule. But, getting back to why I'm here—do you see why I'm not sure how to deal with Arden when it comes to using her land?"

Ina snorted. "No one *deals* with Arden Vervain. Just like every other problem you've brought to me, you're missing something. Only this time…it's a pretty big something."

"Like what?"

"Arden isn't your problem. Arden can be a means to an end. The problem is finding out who is doing this and locating the exchanged children. Medbh suggested it's a creature trying to get someone's attention," Ina narrowed her eyes. "That's a pretty detailed *suggestion*. Think about it. Changelings are pretty specific to Faerie lore. Even the most ignorant Cowen out there has pretty much heard of a Changeling and knows the tale of Faeries stealing children and leaving a fake child in their place. So…whose attention are they trying to get?"

I was already ahead of her. "An actual Faerie's attention. Someone from *Alfheim*."

"Right. So if Arden gives you permission to use sacred or consecrated ground, my question to Silver wouldn't be if she knew who was using the power, but what other Faerie creatures were living in New Orleans. Any of the queens would know."

Something glittered in Ina's eyes but I wasn't quite sure why. I'd used her as a sounding board so many times in my life; I trusted the process enough to know eventually the pieces would fall into place. Or at least, land with resounding thuds. I didn't know what I'd do without Ina.

My phone buzzed and I sat forward and dug it out of my jeans. It was a text from Kyle. "Eh…Kyle's ready and it's already been over an hour. I'm sure his aunt gets snippy if she's kept waiting." I stood and Grey stood with me. She had meandered back into the main part of the house, her nails clicking on the worn hardwood floors.

Ina set her cup down and stood to walk me out. At the door she put her hands on my shoulders. "Bring Ivan to me. I want to talk to him. Test him, if he'll agree. If he really can see Arcane Magic, it'll be a Gift that could protect all of you," she kissed my forehead. "And keep his secret from Arden. For now. At least until we can test what his limits are."

"Oh, I already figured Arden was the last person I wanted looking into Ivan. She already treats her own blood harshly just because he's a Hedge Witch. I can't even imagine how she'd take to a Witch that worked in the Cyber World."

We said goodbye. Me with a half-hearted promise to stop by during her party that night. Really…I would rather pull my fingernails out with pliers than sit around and make nice-nice with people who'll never quite understand the world around them.

Grey sat on the sidewalk as I removed the tarp and wadded it back up before I put it in the locker. It hadn't rained yet, but the sky was a bit darker and the air had a different feel.

I fastened my seatbelt as Grey jumped into her position in back. "Feels weird out here, Grey. Like something's…coming."

She *wuffed* in agreement as I pulled the Jeep out into the street and headed to Kyle's apartment.

SEVEN

Arden Vervain's Garden house was in the same neighborhood as Anne Rice's former home. It stood, like all the other homes in the district, as a testament to the size and majesty of Southern Antebellum. Arden's home owned a street corner, surrounded by a black iron fence and thick shrubbery. Both acted as a deterrent for intruders as well as onlookers.

The sidewalk entrance placed the visitor at the mercy of the house's immensity and grandeur. The three of us had been inside this house only once when we came to ask for Arden's help. We had breezed past the antique furniture, Persian rugs and flickering gas lighting along the walls to the back patio where dark red tile surrounded a rectangular pool. Palms and more shrubbery, including tropical, flowering plants had added to the ambience that day.

Arden owned three properties in New Orleans. The largest was her country home, located in the swamps south of the city. The closest I'd come to that home was the night I made that fateful deal with the new Obsidian Queen, Brendi.

Her other property was a mystery. It was rumored anyone who found it was never heard from again.

But that was all it was, a rumor. Or so I hoped.

Arden had old money, and some she'd made herself. I never looked into how she made it. I figured the less I knew the better. I didn't like her. Didn't trust her. She put one of my people into a coma—albeit by accident. She was like her home and gardens.

Beautiful and deadly.

There were four official covens in New Orleans and Arden's was the largest. My little group of three didn't count, though we did make a blip on the radar from time to time. Arden had suggested that we would be smart to associate ourselves with her coven.

Minus Ivan.

I told her to get fucked.

Kyle's relationship to Arden was a complicated one. Kyle was Arden's sister's youngest. The only boy in the family and the only one of the three children to possess the God Mother's Gift. But Arden and her little group of Elders, old biddies with drawn faces and garish taste in clothing, believed the magic of ritual, the specialty of the Hedge Witch, was the right of females, not males. The fact he had the power and his sisters didn't had never ingratiated him to his siblings.

I met Kyle the night before those same sisters, along with his mother, decided to take Kyle's magic from him. Lucky for him and unlucky for them, I was aware of their plot. They no longer lived in Louisiana and they dared never return. That incident put me on the map for Arden and her group and they gave me a wide birth.

Kyle and I had been together ever since, and I'd watched him hone and sharpen his magic. I paid for the tattoos on the backs of his hands and the ones on the tops of his feet, which he used as magical tools. Kyle was more than his aunt realized, but it still didn't mean the two got along.

My hair stuck out with the electric current running through the ground as we got out of my Jeep and Grey jumped out of the back to follow at my side. Heat lightning illuminated the October evening, making the overhanging Spanish moss covered oaks look all the more imposing. It was all an ill effect that didn't impress me.

What Ivan did today? Now *that* impressed me.

I had explained this new power of Ivan's to Kyle on the drive and he seemed stoked about it. As soon as we were done at Arden's, I wanted to get back to Ivan and ask him if he saw the same red worms around Medbh. She didn't emit the same smell as Arcane Magic did, but that had to be what kept her locked in her head.

The large oak door opened as we entered. We were greeted by four women of all races and shapes, all dressed in black robes. They went over the rules of the house and made us take our shoes off. I had to leave my guns by the front door. I ordered Grey to stay there and not let anyone touch them. She *woofed* at me once and then turned her glare on the others.

A red-haired siren in a green robe led us through the house along the same path we'd taken months before. Not much had changed. Antique Victorian furniture, garish red velvet upholstery, matching wallpaper and ugly china in the cabinets. The main parlor still reminded me of a Wild West bordello.

We were led back to the patio again to the pool. Arden had a roof and screened in walls added since our last visit. But I could still see the impending storm.

Seated in a fan-backed chair like the kind I used to see in old *Tarzan* movies sat Arden Vervain. She wore a black gown and black slippers. Her hair, blacker and longer than my own, fell down around her shoulders and spilled onto her lap. Silver chains and amulets decorated her neck and hung in descending order. I counted two pentagrams, three ankhs, a Star of David and a cross. None of them were spelled or charmed. They were all for show.

"That will be all, ladies."

Our escorts bowed and left the room.

Once the door closed, Arden let loose a long sigh, ripped off the wig to reveal her natural shoulder-length, dark brown hair. She stood and slipped off the black robe and tossed it on the chair with the wig. Beneath it she wore a gray pantsuit and white shirt. The chains came off all at once from a single, large clasp in the back.

"You have a meeting today?" Kyle asked as Arden dropped the heavy jewelry in the chair with the robe and wig.

She held out her arms and stretched before she answered. "Yes. With several of the other leaders as well as some scattered occultist groups. And they were all concerned about what happened at your shop today, Samantha." Arden went to a nearby table laden with crystal decanters and a matching ice bucket. She pulled out a highball glass, tossed ice in it and poured herself a bourbon. "Anyone thirsty?"

"No thanks," I said as I stood and waited.

"Of course not." She tossed the shot down and then set the glass on a side table beside the fan back chair. "Remind me again where your cheap little shop is, *shugar*? Somewhere between the cathedral and *Club Hell*?"

I met Arden's ornery tone with one of my own. "*Club Hell* is on St. Peter Street. *Bell, Book and Candle* is on Bourbon, down from LaFitte's Blacksmith Shop and Bar. But then, if you really were on top of the magical machinations of this town like you claim, you'd know that. You'd also already know exactly what happened and wouldn't be wasting our time asking us."

"They still don't use lights in that bar?"

"No. They don't." I licked my lips as I tried to keep my frustration in check. "Miss Vervain—"

"Arden. I told you to call me Arden the last time."

"You told me a lot of things the last time we met. And I said some things as well."

"Oh, I don't regret anything I say, *shugar*. I meant it when I said it, but I am inclined to change my mind later. Little bit of ruckus at that shop of yours."

"The ruckus didn't start at my shop. It ended there with a child putting a cinder block through my window."

"How old was the child?"

Kyle spoke up. "Six."

Arden's dark brows arched. "And she lifted a cinder block?"

"Twice."

"She also killed a man and gnawed on her own mother's neck," I rubbed at my face. "We didn't do anything to bring them there."

She turned and faced us. "I know what people told me happened, but I prefer to hear from the mouths of those who were there. There's nothing nefarious about my asking the questions, Samantha."

"You'll excuse me if I don't trust you."

Arden looked past us. "I take it the Dianic member of your little group declined my invitation."

"I told him not to come. Like I said, I don't trust you." And now that it was evident Ivan could see Arcane Magic, I somehow trusted Arden even less around him. "Miss Vervain, I'm assuming Kyle filled you in on what we would like to do on a small section of your land? Possibly the same patch we used before?"

"You're never going to forgive me for that little misunderstanding with the Dianic," Arden said, ignoring what I'd just said, referring back to Ivan.

"You put him in a coma."

"That was an accident…which still baffles me. How exactly did I do that?"

"Doesn't matter. He recovered just fine."

Arden walked around her fan-back chair. "Yes, my nephew informed me of your request."

"Miss Ver—" I stopped. "Arden. We need to talk to Medbh's sister."

"Tzariene. I know of her. You do realize she's crazier than Medbh."

I thought they were all crazy but I didn't want to stand and debate this. I went over the events that happened at the shop, shortening a few things and completely leaving out what I knew Ivan had done.

Once I finished she narrowed her eyes. "So the little detective is still here. This *Cruise* character?"

"Crwys. He works for the NOPD."

"And his Vampire partner?"

"Here as well. Crwys said he smelled Arcane Magic, and honestly," I glanced back at Kyle who remained quiet. "We did too. Only I didn't know that was what I smelled. I haven't been exposed to Arcane enough to know that. When we asked Medbh if that's what it was, she confirmed it."

"So she told you to talk to Tzariene?"

"Not in so many words. But she did admit having a suspicion the Changelings weren't being used by the Faerie."

"Of course she'd say that. It throws suspicion off of herself," she moved back to the table and poured herself another drink.

"Miss Vervain—"

"Are you fucking deaf? My name is Arden." Her voice grew in

volume and I felt her presence. And when I say I felt it, I mean I *felt* it. Don't get me wrong, Arden was powerful. Her magic was strong and she had the swamp and its water as her power base even this far away from it. "You can do your ritual, but only under my conditions, and for a price. The Circle will be drawn by my people and I will be present during the communication," she pursed her lips into a pouty smile. "And one more thing. I want the head."

I blinked. "The head? You mean Medbh?"

"What other head is there? I want it. You give me the head first and then we call Tzariene."

"Aunt…what do you want the Sidhe's head for?" Kyle spoke up. I moved close to him just in case the wacko went wicked.

"Because *I* should have it." She didn't look at Kyle when she talked. She looked at me. "I am the Queen of this town and that thing is dangerous. It should be under *my* care, under *my* guard."

I had wondered for a time if this was the underlying reason for her dislike of me. I possessed something she wanted. Arden had seen the head only once eight months ago and it had remained silent in her presence. Medbh refused to talk though everyone else could hear her.

I knew then the bitchy little ceramic queen was fucking with the bigger bitchy queen. Medbh didn't like Arden. And Arden didn't like Medbh.

Arden was willing to contact the other Faerie Queen just to get a hold of the head, not to help in getting rid of the Changelings. I made the decision right then that we didn't need to talk to Tzariene. Based on what Ina had suggested, I needed to talk to Medbh again, and I needed to talk to Crwys, even though I didn't want to. The key to finding out why the Changelings were out and killing and how to stop them wasn't here with Arden.

Not like this.

"The answer is no, Arden. Merry meet." I turned, grabbed Kyle by the upper arm, and half dragged him with me back into the house to the front door. Grey wagged her tail as I approached and then growled at Arden as she followed us.

"Don't walk out on me, Samantha. That head should be in a

safer place and not locked up in some shack. It's dangerous, and the whole magical community wants it either moved or gone."

I finished putting my boots on and threw my finger in Arden's face. "*You* are the reason they know it exists. If you'd kept that big mouth shut, this kind of bullshit wouldn't be impeding our real work. We're born into this world to protect it, not argue about it. That head is fine where it is. We've got something bigger and badder out there exchanging children for Changelings and they are killing people. So why don't you put your great coven together and do something worthwhile for once and find out where the real kids are!" I turned and headed out the door.

I walked fast, my hair flying behind me as the heels of my boots struck the concrete walkway. I was pissed. I was angry and I was trying really hard not to cry. I just wanted to run by my place, grab a bag and find Robin. I wanted sex. And I wanted it now.

My phone rang as I got to my Jeep. I dug it out of my pocket and saw it was Robin's number. In fact it looked like he'd called me a dozen times. I forgot phones didn't work in Arden's house. Grey jumped in the back and Kyle got in the driver's seat after I tossed him the keys.

I slipped in and hit redial. "Hey babe—what's wrong?"

I barely understood his voice as he said, "It's Rose. Oh my God, Sam. Kathy attacked Rose. My niece grew teeth and claws and attacked her mother!"

EIGHT

When I arrived at Tulane University Medical Center, Rose was already in surgery. Robin met us at the nurse's station and we gave each other a tight, heartfelt hug. When I pulled back to look at him I was shocked. He was pale, his face gaunt and his usually perfect hair was mussed. I could see he'd been raking his fingers through it, like he always did when he was upset. He had blood on his cheek and neck and on his shirt, but he assured me it was all Rose's blood.

"The doc said Kathy nicked a main artery when she bit Rose. Just a bit deeper…she'd have bled out."

"Where are the kids?" Kyle was lucid enough to ask the right questions. I was still too close and in a sort of shock.

"Marly's with my mom, but Kathy…" his beautiful face scrunched up as his voice cracked and a tear dropped from his red-rimmed eyes. "She's dead. I killed her. I didn't know what else to do. She just went crazy at the dinner table. One minute we were talking and laughing and the next Kathy was up on the table, a knife in her hand. She backhanded her sister, swiped the knife at me and jumped on her mother. It all happened so fast."

I put my hands on his chest. "Just take a deep breath, okay? That's good, and another, and tell me where Kathy's body is now."

"The morgue I guess. I got the knife from her and stabbed her in the neck," he put a blood stained hand to his face and his tears ran pink. "I just….oh my God, Sam…what the hell happened?"

I pulled him close to me again. He was shaking from head to

toe and I assumed it was from adrenaline and shock. Robin was going to collapse at any minute if he didn't relax. I guided him to a nearby bench in the waiting room as Kyle ran to get coffee.

With his head on my shoulder, I had to think of the ramifications of this. His niece attacked his sister in exactly the same way the Changelings were attacking. Without seeing Kathy, I had to assume she was a Changeling too, which just put a personal stamp on this crisis for me. I was concerned earlier, but now I was determined to find out where the exchanged children were being held, and who was holding them.

Kathy was the one with the God Mother's spark.

If they were somewhere in New Orleans, this was doable. If they were in *Alfheim*, *eeh*—it was doable. But I didn't want to do it. I really didn't want to go into Faerie Land.

I really needed to talk to Tzariene. But I wasn't about to relinquish Medbh into the hands of a woman who might very well use the Sidhe's severed head for nefarious purposes. I didn't have proof that Arden was a bad woman, regardless of her reputation. But I had my doubts about her daily morals and noticed how they seemed to change to fit the circumstance.

"It's going to be okay, babe."

"No," he said, his voice muffled as spoke against my neck. "Nothing's ever going to be the same again."

A double door opened down the hall and a man in scrubs stepped out. Blood decorated the front of his shirt and he wore a grim look on his face. Robin stood, telling me that was the doctor. I stood up as well; ready to hear the verdict when my phone rang. I stepped away and looked at the face.

Any other time I would have ignored Crwys's badly timed call, but given what we were up against, he might have news. I held the phone out and excused myself as the doc pulled Robin away. "This better be good."

"Did you know the grocer was *the* High Witch?"

I had to realign my paradigm for a second so I could register what he just asked me. "You're joking, right? Higgins was *the* High Witch? I didn't even know he was a Witch."

"I know! Which makes him a great High Witch. Or made."

I still had to think on that. After a few seconds the reality of that statement hit home. "Shit…the Changeling killed the High Witch."

"Keep up, Hawthorne. Higgins was well liked among the whole magic community in the quarter. My intel says the Elders had a meeting this afternoon about his death and from what I'm hearing…they want answers."

A group that had a meeting. Kyle asking Arden if she had a meeting came back to me. So did all that regalia she'd been wearing. It was obvious she didn't dress that way around her coven, and she was an Elder. "Fuck. They had their meeting at Arden's place." I gave him a brief run-down of our meeting with Arden and her sudden request for Medbh's head.

"It makes sense they'd blame Medbh. Changelings are Faerie business and there's a Sidhe head in your basement. They're following a trail, I'm just not sure it's the right one."

"Damn that woman," I said in a less than low tone. A few nurses and a hot orderly passed by, giving me a wide birth. "I haven't told anyone about Medbh's head. Neither has Ivan or Kyle. But Arden's been running her mouth."

"She might be gunning for the High Witch position, Sam. She already calls herself the Witch Queen of New Orleans. If she were elected to the head position, it would guarantee her that power. And by giving the Elders the head of a Sidhe? But not just any Sidhe, the former Obsidian Queen, I'd bet that election would be in the bag."

That. Bitch.

"Where are you?" Crwys asked.

I realized he didn't know, so I filled him in on what'd happened.

"That's seven Changelings."

"I'm aware of that. So where are the real kids? Are they all in *Alfheim*?"

"We should have asked Medbh that. Look, we're going to have to find a way to speak to Tzariene to see if she knows anything. There's no telling how long these Changelings have been living their counterparts' lives," he paused. "You do realize Robin's sister's not going to survive this. Not if that thing bit her."

"The doctor's talking to Robin right now. It looked like he was getting some good news." I turned to make sure Robin was still there.

And he was. He'd turned to his right to speak to the doc and I saw his left side for the first time. His bloodied shirt moved as he held up his arms as if gesturing and I saw the surgical tape and gauze of a bandage.

"Sam? You still there?"

I swallowed as I stared at the thread-woven piece of material, taped with such care and precision to my lover's side, just below what looked like the trailing edges of long, deep scratches. "Crwys…is it just biting that feeds the toxins?"

"No. It's any kind of contact that'll flay skin. Biting, gnawing, clawing."

I put my hand to my mouth just as Robin turned to me and smiled. He waved me over. I lowered my hand and nodded. "I gotta go."

"What is it? What's wrong?"

"I'll meet you at the shop." I disconnected and slipped my phone into my back pocket with shaking hands as I joined my lover. I put my hand over the bandages and inhaled deep.

He winced and just there on the edge, like a fleeting memory was the rotting, pungent smell of Arcane Magic.

NINE

Kyle met me outside the hospital. The woman who appeared outside my shop, the first victim we knew, had died. Her body was on its way to the morgue.

I didn't say much in the Jeep. Grey moved between the two front seats and put her head on my shoulder. She licked my ear a few times, and I absently reached back to scratch her neck.

Tomorrow would be Halloween. All soul's night.

And by tomorrow night my boyfriend would be as dead as the rest of the Changelings' victims. What I couldn't wrap my head around was *why*. Why were they all coming to life at once? Like sleeper agents set to kill, all activated at the same time. What was the purpose?

Ina's words kept tumbling around me as well. I should focus on whose attention the wielder of the Changelings was focused on. Otherwise, none of this would ever make sense.

The sun set while I was in the hospital. We sat in the Jeep under the twilight part of the day, in the parking lot under threatening clouds, but still no rain. I fished my phone out of my back pocket.

Ina answered on the fifth ring. "Hey…everything go well with Arden?"

I could hear people's voices, soft music and laughter. I imagined Ina's house was warm and full of companionship by now. I gave her a fast recap of what happened at Arden's.

"Sam, what else is wrong? You sound just a little off."

"I don't…I don't want to talk about it right now. But I need a favor. It's a crazy idea, but it might help us."

"Sure. Just come on over and we can talk."

"I have Kyle with me."

"Bring him. And call Ivan to come as well. If this involves magic, you three must continue working together to forge your coven bonds."

I called Ivan and told him to meet us at Ina's in half an hour.

The house was lit up just as I imagined it would be. My parking space was still available and we wasted no time getting inside as thunder cracked the otherwise calm night.

There were seven students in the house with Ina, along with one of the other teachers, an older woman I knew as Venus. She was like the students, all children of the God Mother, all carrying a single Dianic Gift.

Once Ivan arrived, I spelled out my idea in the herb room and got everyone's opinion. Ina was okay with giving it a try, more than ready to throw her students into the deep end of real, working magic. So we filed back into the main room where everyone waited patiently, some whispering among themselves.

The boy to girl ratio was nearly even, which surprised me. Once everyone gave us their magical names—a name they chose to be called in Ina's house—she turned the floor over to me.

I felt a bit nervous standing in front of everyone's wide eyes. They were all dressed for a party in nice clothes and shoes, while I stood in my usual uniform of boots, jeans and a black tank top. Luckily, I'd remembered my leather jacket, but it was in Ina's front closet. And she had my weapons tucked away.

"Is that a *real* wolf? 'Cause you know that's illegal to keep a real wolf as a pet."

The woman who asked the question called herself Arwen. Why was it always the Stevie Nicks wannabes that flocked to Ina? Arwen was taller than me, but I'm not exactly a giant at five foot seven. She had honey-wheat colored hair, all pulled up into an exquisite French braid, large blue eyes and flawless skin. She wore several layers of flowy skirts and coverings and had silver rings on her toes.

I don't know why, but Arwen set off all my *don't likes*. "Grey is not my pet. She's my familiar. As for whether or not she's a wolf, that's not what's important."

"She's beautiful."

That was Greysmoke, a young brunette in her mid-twenties, with bright brown eyes and a half crooked smile that I actually liked. Everyone focused on Grey where she sat at my feet and she appeared to be taking the attention in stride.

Ina stepped in and held up her hand. "I need everyone to focus. And listen carefully to Sam and I. What we're going to do hasn't been done with Dianic Magic, though the outcome shouldn't be any different." Well, that announcement quieted the room. "Samantha and her friends, Kyle and Ivan, need to talk to someone in the Circle. So we're going to draw down the moon for them and make it possible."

Wider eyes and open mouths.

Then, "But…can't the three of them do it themselves?" Arwen's whiny voice made the hairs on the back of my neck bristle.

I answered that one. "Yes, we could. But because everyone here works the Circle in the back yard on a regular basis, I think the potency of the magic we need would be better if it was cut from your imagination."

This was the idea that came to me while sitting in the Jeep outside the hospital. The need to talk to Tzariene was key in discovering if there were other Faeries in New Orleans and we needed consecrated ground to do it. I realized then that Arden didn't have the only consecrated, magically operational ground in the city. In fact, I'd just visited such a place earlier in the evening.

Ina had agreed with it. She knew summoning Tzariene wouldn't be dangerous for the casters—the ones inside the Circle asking the questions were the ones at risk. What concerned me was what price Tzariene would ask for the answer.

Everyone seemed excited, except for Arwen, though she followed the group as they gathered outside in Ina's back yard. In the dark, under lit torches and paper lanterns, the Circle looked ethereal. When Ina moved to this house, I helped her work the Circle on Sabbats and Moons, and physically built the area when I was home from college.

Nine feet in diameter, the center of the Circle was set with a permanent fire pit. Around the edge were tiles of yellow and red in the patterns of flames. At each of the four directions tall stones were set to represent the orientation and their corresponding Elements. North for Earth, east for Air, south for Fire and west for Water. The altar was set in the north. Knee-high shrubbery outlined the Circle space and kept everything nice and neat.

The group had the altar ready and wood in the fire within a half hour after the proposed impromptu ritual. Kyle, Ivan and myself had a quick meeting in the herb room to go over what we needed to say.

"I remember the meeting you had with Brendi," Kyle said. "We don't want another bargain like that."

"Are you sure she'll ask for something in return?" Ivan looked at each of us. He'd changed into a black hoodie, jeans and boots. His lip ring really shined in the candlelight. "And does it have to be a promise like you made Brendi?"

I shook my head. "It's what ever they fancy at the time."

Ina came in with a clay pitcher and set it on the table. "For what it's worth, my experience has always been that the easiest way to get through a Faerie deal is to sweeten it. This is a pitcher of well-blended honey and milk. I've also added catnip for potency. I think you should offer it before she thinks of something," she looked at Ivan. "And I think you should do it."

Ivan took a step back. "Me? Why Me?"

"Because you pose the least magical threat." Ina reached out and put a hand on Ivan's shoulder. They were about the same height. "Ivan, Sam told me what you did in the shop. That's an incredible Gift and I want to work with you on sharpening it. You could be such a valuable asset to her—hell—to any Witch in the city. To actually see Arcane?"

"But...I don't know if it's a fluke or a one time thing."

"That's why you need to be the one to make the offer. Tzariene is, for all practical purposes, composed of this magic. Arcane is what binds the Demon Realms together. The light, the dark and *Alfheim*. She'll let you close because she can't sense your magic."

"But if it wasn't a fluke, then I should be able to see the Arcane."

"Exactly."

I wasn't all that happy about putting Ivan into Tzariene's line of sight. Hell, I wasn't that happy about putting myself there. What if she thought of taking me and handing me over to Brendi just to make nice with the new Obsidian Queen?

Ick…stop thinking so negatively. You're just worked up about Robin. I looked at Kyle and Ivan. "Ready?"

"Sure," Kyle said.

"No," Ivan answered. "But I'll do my best."

Ina smiled. "Venus is leading the build right now. The Circle's been cut. I'll come get you when they're ready. Oh, and you remember the challenge response?"

Circles were created by the gestalt of the Circle's participants. The theory was that everyone had the same visual, knew the same words, and did everything the same way. Cowens wouldn't have the same feeling involved in cutting a Circle the way the God Mother's children would. The children felt the cut of the athame into the ground and the spherical shape of the sacred space as it was locked into place.

And from the buzzing that started in the back of my head, these students of Ina's were good at what they did. I knew the second that Circle was set to the stones.

Grey sat outside the Circle, a happy wolf watching along the edge. But I knew from the perk of her ears she was listening. And watching. And ready to tear this queen a new asshole if needed…or bite her head off.

Ten minutes later we were led to the Circle, rightly challenged and then led in around the fire pit. The flames crackled and popped and I felt the old, familiar energy re-awaken memories of nights in robes, the smell of burning wood and the musty scent of incense.

On Ina's command, everyone turned and faced the outside of the Circle. They were to keep the Circle up and listen, but not look. If they looked, Ina would know, and they would be warlocked. She didn't want them getting any funny ideas about calling up Faerie Queens and asking favors.

The three of us formed a triangle in the south quadrant. We each recited our part three times and waited.

A tall, thin pillar of white smoke appeared in the center. It moved and writhed and spun until it finally took form. I'd seen Tzariene before. Kyle and Ivan hadn't. And it was obvious in their expressions and Kyle's gasp.

Tzariene was tall, with white skin and black hair. Her eyes were coal black points on her delicate face and moved to each of us. Her fingers were long, elegant and fussed with the flowing, almost smoky texture of her gown.

Her most striking feature was the great horns protruding from her head, like the branches of a great oak.

I noted the smell. The same as earlier in the day.

Arcane.

I looked at Ivan. He was staring wide-eyed, but there was no mistaking the look of revulsion in his expression. When he put his hand to his head, I knew he was *seeing* Arcane.

"Well, this is a pleasant surprise, Samantha. Brendi will be very upset to hear you've called upon me and not her," Tzariene's voice was light and airy, and yet deep and seductive. "And I love upsetting that woman. So, shall we invite her as well just to make this interesting?"

TEN

That comment blew any fears of being traded off to Brendi out of the water. I stepped forward and bowed before I turned and gestured for Ivan to follow me. "I think it would be best to leave Brendi in the dark. This way, you will have knowledge she doesn't."

Ivan brought the pitcher of milk and honey and offered it to her on bended knee. "My Silver Lady, we offer you this milk and honey in exchange for the answer to a question that will benefit both our people."

I held my breath and watched Tzariene. I was ready to act in case she pulled anything with Ivan. I was pretty sure she couldn't sense Ivan's Gift, but I was also a guardian, a protector by birthright.

Tzariene's smile was dazzling, except for the rows of needle-point teeth. What was it with Faeries and their teeth? She took the pitcher from Ivan, sniffed it, nodded and handed it off to someone we couldn't see.

Tzariene stood in two worlds. Her own, and ours. They couldn't see us, nor us them.

"Such a beautiful offering, Samantha. What is this one's name?"

"We call him Daisuke," I said, blurting out a name that just fit his look. Something she wouldn't question. Faeries liked using names to gain power, and so far they didn't know Kyle's name and they wouldn't know Ivan's if I had anything to do with it. They knew mine because of my deal with Brendi. But while that deal was in place, using my name for gain wasn't allowed.

Sometimes dealing with the Faerie was just too damn complicated.

Tzariene slowly nodded and turned back to me. "Offering is accepted. For a single question. But I would like to know the nature of the summons."

I told her as quickly as I could, recapping what had happened in the shop, the other Changelings, and Medbh's suspicions. It was common knowledge in *Alfheim* that Medbh's head lived in this world. Funny how they were okay with that. Apparently, Medbh's reputation was so bad they *wanted* her in another world.

I didn't know what kind of response I would get from Tzariene, but the expression she gave me was a little freaky. Somewhere between livid and pissed off.

"No other is allowed the use of Faerie Magic. If there is someone using our ways then I would very much like a word with this individual."

That would be bad for them. A word with Tzariene was usually a nice long stay in her dungeon.

She straightened. "If you had not brought me the milk and honey, I would demand ownership of this person. But, as it is, the bargain is struck. Ask your question."

I licked my lips. I could feel the strain of keeping the Circle up starting to wear on the Dianics. "Are there any other Faerie living in New Orleans, other than Medbh's head?"

Tzariene closed her eyes for a few seconds, then, "No. The only Faerie in your world is my sister," she showed her teeth again. "I would give you a word of advice, Samantha. Order my sister to tell you the truth. And if she keeps silent, burn patchouli."

I blinked. "Patchouli?"

"Yes. She hates the smell." Tzariene gave a low bow and vanished. The smell of Arcane lingered for a second then disappeared as well.

The group took the Circle down and we all moved back into the house. The members immediately took their leave and as they were saying goodbye to one another, the four of us huddled in the herb room once again.

I moved close to Ivan. "Tell me what you saw."

His eyes grew to the size of goose eggs. "Sam—it was everywhere.

It wasn't just worms that pulsed and moved. I could see the door that woman stood in the middle of. It was like some weird, long oval mirror. She had one foot in our world and one foot in her own, and the stuff… it swirled around her in mixing colors of black and red. When she moved it sparkled like tiny stars in the black," he paused and made a face. "And it smells so bad."

"I was wondering if your sense of smell of it would be stronger since you can detect and actually see it," Ina put her hand on her worktable. "The black and the red are interesting. Sounds like a blending of powers or magic."

"That pitcher," Ivan said. "When I handed it to her I watched it transform from just a pitcher into this magnificent silver flask made of the same sparkling stuff. And when someone else touched it, it transformed from the stars into the black misty stuff. I don't know if there's a correlation or not, but I sort of saw it as a transmutation. When the queen took it, she changed its core from something in this world, to something in her own."

I looked at Ina. She looked at me.

Kyle whistled. "Dude…this new power of yours is freakier than the usual."

"Yeah," Ivan said and put his hand to his head. "It's also giving me a headache."

"Food will help that." Ina patted the table as she straightened. "But first," she said as she turned and went to one of the drawers in the shelving. She pulled out a long handled knife and set it on the table. "What does this look like to you?"

Ivan frowned. "It's covered in those red worms. What is it?"

I looked at the knife and all I saw was a knife. "You can see those same worms, the ones you saw attacking me and Kyle, on the knife."

"They're not just on the knife. They're *in* the knife."

I started to put my hand on the knife, but Ina grabbed it and shoved it back in the drawer. I stared at her. "What the hell? You have an Arcane knife."

"No, it's not Arcane. Not originally. I just needed to know something about it. So, let's get everyone some stew and," she said as she turned and stopped. "Arwen—what are you still doing here?"

I spun and saw the irritating blond on the other side of the herb room's entrance. She had her coat on and her purse over her shoulder. Just how long had she been standing there? And what the hell did she hear?

"I didn't know if you wanted me to lock up," Arwen's gaze slipped from Ina to Ivan in the back of the room. "The fire pit's out and the instruments have been put away."

"Yes, yes. Lock up. And thank you for your time, Arwen. Now get home and get some sleep. Tonight's work was exhausting." Ina threw me a worried glance before she led the young girl back into the house to the front door.

"I don't like her," Kyle spoke up. He'd been oddly quiet for the night.

"Me either."

After the house was locked up, and all three of us were full of Ina's wonderful stew, she shuttled us upstairs to bedrooms, insisting it would be safer to stay with her for the night, and not return to the broken magic shop.

I'd changed into a pair of soft cotton loungers and a threadbare *Inferno* t-shirt I kept in my room upstairs. Grey, full from her own bowl of stew, snored on top of the bed as I crept back downstairs. I summoned a little Fire Salamander to light my way. Cowens and other Witches would use a candle or a flashlight. Elementals? Well…we're just wired different. And though I wouldn't have brazenly used my magic in my own home or shop like that, I felt safe at Ina's. We all did.

That and I thought the Salamanders were cute and I wanted the company. Don't let anyone ever tell you different, but Elementals had their own personalities. Some were quite boring and all play by the rules. Fire Elementals? Way too much fun.

I stepped into the herb room and the Salamander immediately started dancing in his tiny pool of light. Whatever was in the room— he didn't like it. How did I know it was a he? Did I look to see if it had the right parts? No. Fire was a male Element, so most of the time the creatures I asked to help me were male.

I assumed the presence of Arcane set it off. Which meant the knife was still there. I opened the drawer. The shiny metal blade reflected the Salamander's light. The hilt felt cool in my hand. Nothing tingled. Nothing felt wrong about the blade as I lifted it out of the drawer and turned to hold it up to the Elemental's light.

I instantly recognized it as an athame. The symbol of a Witch's will and intent. These blades were consecrated and often used to focus power, but they never drew blood. If that ever happened, even by accident, the blade was unconsecrated and buried at a crossroads for a hundred years.

"It was your mother's."

I yelled out at Ina's voice and nearly dropped the knife on my bare foot. That would have been a very bad thing, not to mention excruciatingly painful. I set the knife on the table and stepped back. "I—damn I'm sorry, Ina. I just wanted to see it. You pulled it away so fast—" and then what she said sunk in. "My mother's?"

"Yes." Ina wore a long gown of soft blue beneath a warm, fuzzy bathrobe. She had matching blue slippers on her feet and picked up the knife. "She used this as her athame all the years I knew her."

I always knew Ina and my mom had been friends, though she never talked about my mom much. I assumed that was because my dad always got upset when we did. He never liked her job as a detective, and begged her to quit till the day it killed her.

The only real things I knew about my mother's magical life were that she was an Elemental like me, and that she was a good Tracker. Like me. And that I looked a lot like her.

I focused on the athame in her hand. "But…why do you have it? Aren't magical tools deconsecrated and buried when their wielders die? And why does it have Arcane in it?"

Ina shook her head as she returned the athame to the drawer. "Those are all good questions, Samantha. And you'll have answers when you're ready. Just know for now there is an answer that makes sense." She turned and touched my cheek with the back of her hand. My little Salamander chittered at her and put up his tiny front hands like fists. Elemental entities could also be very protective. "For both of us."

"I don't do cryptic well, Ina. You know that." I moved away from her and my Salamander did as well. I asked him to move higher and illuminate the room. He did, but begrudgingly.

"Why can't you sleep? You have your answer. You need to confront that head again. I've got plenty of patchouli. Take a few sticks of it before you leave in the morning."

I nodded, but my attention wasn't on Medbh or Tzariene or the Changelings. It was focused on that athame.

"You're going to tell me what's eating at you?"

After a few minutes I finally turned and faced Ina. She held her arms open and I knew she sensed I was sad, and needed comfort. So I moved into those arms, reveling in the embrace that had helped me through my mother's death, the throws of puberty and my first love, Henry Akin.

I confided in her about the wound on Robin's side. She listened, and held onto me as I cried. She never said a single word and after a while, I have no idea how long, she pulled back and took my hands in hers. "I can help you, but I can't cure that kind of magic. It's Arcane, so even if I could, to do so would change me, if not kill me." She let go of my hands and moved past me to the shelf and started taking things down. "Grab the mortar and pestle."

"What are you doing?"

"Making a salve. I can stave off the poison. Once it's done, rub it on the scratch as often as you can. I don't know how long it'll work, or if it'll work at all. But I have to try, just like you do. Now, follow my directions as precisely as you can."

With my attention now refocused on Robin, I did what Ina said, all the while trying to puzzle out in my mind why something or someone would want to catch Medbh's attention so bad they felt they had to kill to do it.

ELEVEN

After a solid night's sleep (I slept till nine!), I woke to find Kyle and Ivan had departed hours ago at dawn. Kyle had told Ina they were going to open the shop and clean.

Dedicated employees.

I kissed Ina after enjoying one hell of a breakfast of eggs, toast, biscuits, bacon, sausage and gravy, and drove Grey and myself to the hospital. The sky still threatened rain and the temperature had dropped enough for me to need my jacket. I left my weapons in the lock box with Grey on top of it.

Robin was sleeping in the waiting room, curled up in the farthest corner in the middle of two chairs pushed together. Seriously. Hospitals needed to get it together and have rooms ready for the families for just this kind of emergency.

He lay on his right side, which gave me access to the bandage. Pulling up a chair, I set the glass container with the salve to my right before I pulled Robin's shirt up. The white tape came up with just a bit of coaxing and when Robin stirred I instantly pushed him down into a deeper sleep with a little nudge of Spirit. I wasn't as proficient in this aspect of my Gift, but I was learning the small stuff. Spirit, being the fifth Element, was a combination of the four and not always easy to manipulate.

Making someone sleep—that was easy. Using it to calm an entire auditorium or city?

Nope.

There were three gouges into his side, and the edges of his skin had puckered. I cursed that damn Changeling, even if it did look like Robin's niece, and slathered the salve on liberally like Ina said. The inflammation instantly disappeared and the redness lessened, but the gouges remained.

We didn't know how long it would last, but for now, it would stop the poison from progressing as fast as it normally would.

I closed the glass container and shoved into the pocket of my jacket before I set the bandage back, lowered his shirt, and ran the fingers of my non-salve coated hand through Robin's soft, blond hair.

He stirred and eventually opened his eyes. When he saw me he smiled. But when he remembered where he was, and why he was there, that smile faded and I helped him sit up. "Seeing you is the best thing that's happened to me all night."

I stood and we put the chairs back so we could hug and kiss. He was less inclined on the kissing, insisting he hadn't brushed his teeth. But I didn't care. I just wanted him to hold me.

We spent the rest of the morning in the cafeteria, drinking bad coffee and talking about anything to keep his mind off of his sister. But eventually it had to come back to it and I was gonna make sure I was there for him.

"I can't…" he said in a soft voice as we sat facing each other, our fingers entwined in the center of the table. "I just can't bring myself to believe I killed my niece."

That was what was going to haunt him the most. I could see it. Even if Rose didn't survive, killing wasn't part of Robin's nature. I believe there were souls whose moral compass was skewed the day they were born from the Well of Souls, but there were others who refused to accept the idea of pain and murder. Robin possessed one of these souls. Killing what he believed was his family?

This was going to leave a scar even I couldn't heal.

Robin's suffering reinforced the need to find the exchanged children alive and deliver them back to what was left of their families. "Robin…listen to me," I made sure to gather his gaze with my own. "What happened wasn't your fault. You didn't kill your niece."

"But I did—"

"No. You didn't. The…" I hesitated. What was I going to call it? I couldn't tell him it was a Changeling. "What attacked you and your sister wasn't your niece. Do you understand?"

He narrowed his eyes at me. "Are you trying to say this has to do with the magic stuff?"

"I'm trying to say…" What the hell *was* I trying to say? I recalibrated at light speed. "Things may not be as bad as you think. But just for now…think about Rose, okay? Keep her in your thoughts."

"You know I will. But Sam," he said as he pulled my hands close to him. "You didn't answer me. Does what happened have to do with the magic stuff?"

I swam in his brown eyes. I saw the need there to believe anything that didn't point to himself and killing. The grasping at straws to make sense of what happened to him. Anyone would want that. Anyone would need answers. Just like I needed answers.

And I was going to get them from Medbh.

"I can't say right now. But here," I pulled the glass container from my jacket and put it in his hands. "If you can, in any way, put this on Rose's wounds. It'll help."

"Will it make her live?"

I blinked. "No. But it will help her…it will ease the pain." I wanted to tell him it would slow the poison, but that was more than he needed to know.

He sat back and unscrewed it. It was yellow and had the consistency of Vicks Vapor Rub. "It smells nice."

"It's something my aunt made. All natural. You don't have to do it, but if you want to—"

"No, I'll do it," he closed it and slipped it into his pocket. "I should get back to her. They'll let me in the room now. It's nearly noon."

I needed to go too. I'd left Grey alone too long and it was time to confront Medbh. I had patchouli and a serious case of irritated. We said goodbye at the ICU station and I half ran back to the elevator and then out to the Jeep. Still no rain and Grey was happy to see me.

Traffic was as it always was, but worse. It was Halloween so all the freaks were out, even at mid-day.

Welcome to Bourbon Street, New Orleans.

I pulled the Jeep into the back alley and hit the automatic door. I saw Ivan's truck parked in the back but not Kyle's car. Once inside, every hair I owned stood on end. Something was *wrong*. Grey leapt out of the Jeep and landed on all fours, her teeth bared.

The lights were out in my office and the break room. This wasn't unusual at mid-day, but there should have been a light coming from around the door to the front of the shop.

I could feel the static rising off Grey's body as she stayed close to me, repeatedly bumping into my side. I pulled my guns from my bag and checked the ammo, both physical and magical. I was ready.

The electric kettle was hot, a signal Ivan was in since he drank chai tea all day long. The cup was ready with honey inside, but it hadn't been poured. The bag lay on the counter, unused.

I checked the wards—and found a big 'effing hole!

"Ivan? Kyle?" I called out as I rushed through the door to the front, my weapons ready. Grey followed beside me, growling.

The first thing I noticed was no light coming through the front windows. There were no curtains or blinds on them, so there should at least be the mid-day, monochromatic near-rain color coming through.

Nada. Pitch black.

I stopped just inside, somewhere behind the front counter, as I sent out a detection *feel*. A *feel* for me was like a tendril of myself. An extension of my essence as I used Spirit. I always liked to think of it as a magical drone. It would see and sense danger before it struck because the *feel* was invisible to everyone else. *Unlike* a drone.

:*There's no one else here.*:

Medbh's voice scared the bat-shit out of me. I made a sharp hissing sound as I moved inside, weapons out in front of me, fingers on the triggers. I stepped on glass and knew I shouldn't have. Kyle, Ivan and Robin cleaned up the glass. My *feel* didn't detect any eminent danger and the head was right.

I engaged the guns' safeties, slipped them back into my bag and summoned another Salamander. This one was bigger than the one that came the night before. It started as a sphere of flame the size of a golf ball in my right palm, then grew to the size and shape of a softball as the little creature formed inside. It floated up to the ceiling and illuminated the place enough for us to pick our way around.

"Hey! Anyone here?"

Kyle's voice came from the back. I turned and stood where I was until he showed up as a silhouette in the doorway. "Whoa…what the hell is going on? What's up with the lights? That you, Sam?"

"Where were you?"

"I was out getting lunch," he held up two bags to punctuate his whereabouts. "I left Ivan here. Where is he?"

"I don't know."

"The place feels wrong," Kyle said. "Oh shit…you see that hole in the wards?"

"Yeah I do. Get to the breaker box next to the stairs to the basement." I nudged the tiny Salamander to follow him and it did. It disappeared behind a door and the place went dark again.

Abruptly, the store lights came on and revealed more than just trashed. My store had been trampled.

Fountains lay in pieces all over the place, water pooled on the hardwood. Piles of water soaked books littered the floor as well. Amulets I'd hung from the ceiling were scattered on the floor. The tables were in pieces and part of the counter was caved in.

"The break room wasn't touched," Kyle said as he stepped out of the back. "Want me to go upstairs to your place?"

"It's fine. I already know it is. They weren't looking for anything in my apartment." That's when I saw the broken flat screen monitor. Ivan's phone lay on the floor, smashed. I couldn't sense him in the building, on the block, anywhere within the limits of my Spirit.

"They took Ivan."

"Who?" Kyle came up behind me as Grey put her snout in my hand.

I had a pretty damn good idea who. And I was pissed. Off.

I marched through the break room, flung open the basement

door, and ran down those stairs. I could see the scars on my wards as I approached. Deep gashes where my essence was challenged over and over again as they tried to get to Medbh.

Luckily the bastards failed.

I opened the door to the safe, yanked that goddamn head out and slammed it down on the table in the center of that room. Kyle and Grey came running down after me but stood out of my way. "Who were they?"

The head was shaking. *:A bunch of Witch bitches.:*

I turned to a nearby shelf, grabbed a hammer and struck the damn thing. It broke into five pieces.

Grey barked. Kyle gasped.

As the pieces came back together I pulled a stick of patchouli out of my jacket, summoned a fire spark and lit the end of the stick. Once the pieces fused back together, with more fissures and cracks, I shoved the patchouli into the head's face.

:Why the hell did you do — AAAIIYYEEEE — No! Get that away from me! Foul, foul stuff!:

"I'm going to continue breaking you down and then getting the smell of this herb all inside the pours of that ceramic so that you smell it every waking instant until I get some answers. If karma won't punish you for lying, then I'm going to."

:But I wasn't lying! There were about seven of them. All women, dressed in black like Witchy ninjas. Some were working magic while others were upstairs trashing the place.:

"Why did they take Ivan?"

The head wobbled a bit. *:I got the impression he wasn't supposed to be here. And I think he hurt a few of them, but there were too many. So when they couldn't get to me and he wouldn't give me up, they took him.:*

I held the smoking incense closer. "Why?" I shouted it.

The ceramic head shook even harder and a small piece fell off onto the floor. *:I don't know! I can't read minds, Witch. They didn't say much and they were protected by wards of their own.:*

I lowered my arm. I had a suspicion. "Arden sent them here to steal you so she could gain favor with the Elders."

"Sam," Kyle cleared his throat. "Look, I know you and Arden have this woman-power thing going on. She doesn't exactly get along with everybody. But I don't think she'd do something this drastically stupid if there wasn't a good reason."

"I'll *tell* you the reason," I shouted at him. I was so damn mad. My shop was trashed and that bitch just kidnapped Ivan, the same kid she'd put into a coma. "Because she's a megalomaniac, that's why. She's a woman who'll stop at nothing to actually make herself the Witch Queen of this damn city!"

I sensed someone in the shop. *Two* someones. My little Salamander, which I'd forgotten about and was still floating about upstairs, gave me images of Crwys and Levi as they came in through the front door (oh great that door lock is broken too) and headed down the steps.

Crwys appeared first with Levi behind him. He looked at me, looked at the hammer, saw the incense and held out his hand. "Wait. Don't destroy it."

"She already broke it once," Kyle said. His voice was tight and I was pretty sure he was pissed at me for speaking so badly about his aunt, but let's get real. The woman was a raging lunatic.

I pointed up. "You see what Arden did to my shop? She broke in, destroyed my livelihood and took Ivan. This is kidnapping. I want her arrested and I want Ivan found," then I refocused on Medbh. "Now the truth, you fucking bitch. Were the Changelings created to get your attention?"

A long pause.

This time I hit the head hard with the hammer and held the incense in the pile of ruins while it reformed around it. Surprisingly enough, the stick of burning incense now protruded from the head's mashed up nose with the burning end on the *inside*.

:Get it out!:

"Answer me!" I pulled another stick out, ready to light it up and break that damn head again.

:Yes! She wants my attention because she wants me dead! The Changelings were her idea of telling me she was here and coming for me!:

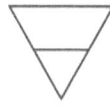

TWELVE

"Who wanted your attention?" I continued holding the hammer over Medbh's head.

When she didn't answer, I raised the hammer with the full intention of smashing the damn thing into pieces small enough to bread chicken with. Medbh Panko.

Crwys grabbed my wrist. I was as surprised by his intervention as much as the heat in his palm. "Stop, Sam. She's not there anymore. Can't you tell?"

"Not there?" I wrenched my wrist free and concentrated on the ceramic head and listened. He was right. There was no echo of Medbh's thoughts, not even the feel of her presence, something I was getting used to. "How is that possible? I thought she was locked into her head?"

"I don't think whatever she is, is gone. I just think she's tuned you out. Maybe passed from the physical to the mental, or even the astral."

I glared at Crwys. "Right. Like you can tell."

He fixed me with that amber red gaze of his. "I can tell many things, Sam. As you damn well know," Crwys's tone wasn't harsh or angry, but it was firm. "Put it back and come upstairs so you can tell me what the hell happened."

I left the incense in the head and just put the whole thing back in the safe without the peanut bag. The ember would snuff itself out once it reached the end of the incense.

Once upstairs, I gave him a quick and dirty review of how I came in to find the devastation, and Kyle backed me up with his version of leaving Ivan to pick up lunch.

Crwys raked his long fingers through his spiky hair, an affectation I knew meant he felt frustration, similar to one of Robin's tells. "I need to call this in. Don't touch anything."

About a half hour later and a pot of coffee, the NOPD was swarming my place. Again. And again Captain Prescott came through my door to the break room table in the back. She leaned forward and pressed her fingertips to the grand oak table. "Nice piece of furniture."

Grey at my feet, made a low *woof* and I leaned down to calm her. I hadn't seen Kyle for a while. Maybe he went home. "Yeah. It is."

"Listen, Miss Hawthorne...I'm sorry about your friend, but what you told Detectives Holliard and Tulouse...I need more concrete proof that it was Miss Vervain who broke into your shop. From the looks of things—"

"Don't you think I know how it looks?" I was harsher than I meant to be, but I was inches from losing my temper. That was something I couldn't let happen.

People would get hurt.

"It looks like someone broke in and I was robbed. But the only thing missing is Ivan. His phone was on the floor, his computer smashed, and his backpack is still under the counter. That says kidnapping?"

"It might, but it doesn't say Miss Vervain is *the* kidnapper," she pursed her lips as she narrowed her eyes at me. "You're more concerned for him than your shop."

"Surprised? He's my friend. I'm pretty much the closest thing to family he's got here. He's also got a cat at home waiting for him." I made myself a mental note to stop by and feed Pyewacket before I...

Before I what? I wasn't going to stay here. Not with a broken shop and bruised wards beneath me. Going to Robin's house wasn't on the table anymore. He'd texted me and said the salve was working wonders. I didn't want to get his hopes up too much. Robin, not understanding magic, would see it as a cure-all and it wasn't. I told him to stay with Rose in the hospital until he had more news. My real thinking was... that if he collapsed from the poison, the hospital was the best place for him to be.

Ina was my only alternative. I needed to get out of here and call her or see her. She'd be just as upset about Ivan as I was, and possibly want to help.

"We'll do what we can, Miss Hawthorne. But I'd keep my accusations against Miss Vervain to myself if I were you." Prescott seemed to notice I wasn't in a talking mood and moved away.

But that didn't stop Crwys from showing up and pouring himself a cup of coffee. "Levi's headed out to talk to some old acquaintances."

"The bloodsucking kind?"

"You know Revenants aren't like that Hollywood shit."

"I don't know anything," I folded my arms on the table and rested my forehead on my forearm. "I'm not seeing something here."

"Like what?" Crwys took the chair opposite of me. I didn't see him, but I could hear him. And feel him. The guy was like a presence I could never shake.

I erased him from my thoughts and refocused on the big question. Why? I had a why for everything. Why was someone, a she, trying to get Medbh's attention? The answer to why anyone would want the former Faerie Queen dead was as myriad as the colors in the rainbow—*everyone* wanted her dead. The line started at my shop. So the next why was…why take Ivan? It was obvious she battered the wards protecting the damned head. Why take a Witch believed to be no more than a Dianic?

Some days I wished this job, this thing that I was, came with instructions. Most Elementals had the advantage of their mother's teaching and guidance. I'd been denied that. And though Ina had done her best, as had my dad in what ways he could, neither of them really understood an Elemental's power.

I wished mom had written it all down. Like a Book of Shadows or something. Most Witches had that. Ina had one. Why didn't my mom?

"How's Robin's sister?"

I took in a deep breath and lifted my head and propped it on my hand. "Ina made a salve to help slow the poison…but she agreed with you. There's no cure."

Crwys slowly nodded, his coffee mug in his hands. Then, "There's no cure in *this* world."

"Well, this is the world that matters. So—" I narrowed my eyes at him. "What are you not saying?"

He moved his index finger around the top of the coffee mug. It was one of my older Renn Faire mugs. Blue. Hand made. "It's all Arcane Magic. Faerie Magic, my magic, Levi's abilities. The poison is Arcane in its makeup because when Changelings are made, they're infused with the poison. But everything in all the worlds has an opposite. Rules of the universe. All poisons have antidotes. It's the nature of their creation. Reverse engineering."

"You're saying…there *is* a cure…only it's an Arcane cure."

"No."

"Crwys, I'm really not in the mood for puzzles."

"If there is an Arcane curse, then there is a counter curse in the opposite. What is opposite of Arcane Magic?"

I sat up. No one had ever asked me that before. Arcane was just something I wasn't ever supposed to touch. "I don't…Crwys, dammit, just spit it out."

"The answer to that is different, depending on what philosopher you read, or what Magician you follow."

I nearly spit at the mention of Magicians. Damn lot of interlopers with no real grasp of how things work. "I don't read Magician crap."

"You should. Many of the great practitioners of magic over the centuries have been members of Magician Orders. Just because Witches and Magicians don't see eye-to-eye in the application of magic—"

I slammed my hands palm down on the table. "Magicians seek to control and dominate the natural world. They're abominations."

Crwys shrugged. "Maybe. But because they don't have those moral codes the way you do, they research and experiment, and you know what else?" he smirked. "They write that shit down because they want the fame and the recognition. Their own hubris is their undoing."

I leaned back. "I think I lost your point. Did you?"

"No. My point is, they *write it down*, Sam."

I stared at him. What…it couldn't be that simple. "You're…you're saying Magicians found a cure and they wrote it down?"

"Yes," he fixed me with his amber red eyes. "There is a cure for the toxin. It was written down centuries ago. A complex spell of Arcane that works as a sort of rewind on the victim. Something a very unhappy mythical wizard discovered somewhere in England a very long time ago."

I continued staring at him. Grey sat up and looked at me, her ears up. "Do you know where it's written?"

"In a book, but I don't know where the book is."

"You're saying there is a book out there with the cure in it."

"There are several books out there, but they're all part of the same original tome. But most Magicians and Witches who tried to use the book have failed because they didn't realize what kind of magic the spells produced."

"Because the spell the Magicians worked were Arcane." I knew this part. All the warnings I'd received through the years about never using Arcane Magic. "Because it changes you."

"Or kills you, like they all found out. This book's got more than just the Changeling's spell in it. There's work on necrification, zombification, exorcism and a guide through the Well of Souls."

"Now you're just playing with me," I fixed him with a very serious look. "'Cause I don't know if necrification is a word."

"It is for what we're talking about," he sipped his coffee again and stared at me.

"Exorcisms? You mean like the kind the Catholic priests do?"

"Far worse. Exorcisms that rend possessing spirits from bodies."

"And this is part of a larger book?"

"It was. A long time ago. But now it's grown on its own and coveted by Magicians the world over."

I ran my hand along Grey's flank. "And you've seen this book."

"Yeah. I have. It's still around. But Sam…even if you had it, you couldn't use it. The spell that would save Robin's sister would inevitably do harm to you, and I can't let that happen."

"Then why tell me about the book?"

"Because you've always been about knowledge. How can you fight something or avoid its pitfalls if you don't know about it? And

I know you would eventually come up with the answer on your own. I just wanted to save you the time and the expense, and the danger of looking for it," he reached out to grasp my other hand. "Look, it's Rose's time. There's nothing you can do to save her. What you have to concentrate on is figuring out who Medbh was talking about and discovering where Ivan is."

I pulled my hand from his. I heard him. I did. But I couldn't move beyond a certain point. "It's…it's not Rose I want to save."

I didn't think I needed to go any further and explain about Robin's wound. And I was right. Crwys gave a low, ragged sigh. "Damn," was all he said as he slumped back in his chair and pushed his still warm coffee away. "I'm sorry, baby. I really am. But…I just can't—"

"You help me find that book, or so help me I will banish your ass back to where you came from."

"You already tried. You can't."

I bored my gaze into his. "I can. All I have to do is find out what you are, and then I can send you back. And you know eventually I'll have your secret."

"Threatening me won't save Robin."

"Tell me, or I'll banish Levi."

Now I'd hit him where it hurt. Levi was more than just a partner. They'd been friends for centuries and would do anything for the other. "You fucking touch him, Witch, and I swear I'll destroy you."

I wasn't afraid of him. Not at that moment. Not when I needed that cure to save Robin's life. Not when I had to face a crazy Witch Queen and the disembodied head of a Faerie. I stood slowly and leaned forward, bracing my fingers on the table. "You are here by *my* permission, Crwys Holliard. You exist in this space because I allow it. The God Mother granted me the Gift that will destroy you and no being from any of the Worlds can stop me or any Elemental Witch. You tell me the name of this book, and where I can find it."

He stood as well and faced me as he leaned in until we were nose to nose. Sexual tension is a lot like anger sometimes. The two seem to engage each other, and my magic loved his. Needed it. Whatever it was.

His eyes burned red and I could feel heat radiating from him.

Beads of perspiration instantly formed on my face, rolled down my cheek. He was challenging me. Daring me.

"Don't test me, Crwys. I will banish Levi. Now tell me."

Grey had been strangely silent until that moment. She began a low growl as she moved under the table and faced Crwys's crotch. I knew what she was doing. I'd taught her the move. He attacks me, and this body, whether it's really his or not, goes through the remainder of its life nut-less.

Crwys made the first move by straightening up. He backed away from the table and then slid his chair under it. "If you go this route, Sam, I can't help you."

"I don't want your help. I never have."

"Fine." He scooped up his cup and poured the coffee in the sink. Then, "You know this book because of its name. It's been the bane of Witches since the stupidity of the Witch Trials. Back in the day, Magicians blamed Witches for their failures. So they wrote a book that served as a blueprint to find Witches, torture them, and kill them."

I felt as if I'd been struck as I leaned against the table. "That can't be right. I have a copy of that book."

"Not the original. This particular volume is the single sticking point between Witches and Magicians. The Witches stole it about two hundred and eighty years ago, and since that time, the Magicians have insisted they return it. The Witches deny it. So the book moves from Elder to Elder, High Witch to High Witch," Crwys rinsed out the cup and set it in the sink. "And now our relationship is over, Miss Hawthorne."

I stood in the break room long after Crwys left the shop. Eventually I went into my office and took down a copy of the book in question and opened it.

So there was an original copy of this monster, and it was possessed by High Witches—

No.

Was it possible? Was this the reason Higgins had been killed and not by a fluke? I yanked my phone out of my pants pocket and dialed Ina's number. "Hey…I need to talk to you."

"Sure. I'm finishing up here. What's this about?"

I looked at the book on my desk. "It's about the truth of the Malleus Maleficarum."

The Witch's Hammer.

THIRTEEN

I made sure the windows were boarded up, again, and the place was secure even through the police tape outside. Again, what I loved about this town was that Cowens wouldn't notice the shop now because I didn't want them to. The NOPD would know what happened there because they were a part of it.

The way the magic worked in New Orleans was a little like having two cities. The one the Cowens saw, and the one we saw. As I drove Kyle and I to Ina's, my shop wasn't in the Cowen world at the moment. It would return when I wanted it to. Passersby would see an empty building for sale.

Taking something out of the Cowen world wasn't always the smartest thing to do. With the place now residing in the one reality also meant I was more visible to the unsavory types, like the Magicians and Sorcerers and what ever nefarious magic benders moved along the streets of New Orleans.

At any other time, I might not have chosen to take my shop off the market, so to speak. But Ina had agreed to talk to me and I felt like time was important. Especially when it came to saving Robin and finding Ivan.

And bringing charges against Arden.

After I told Ina what happened on the phone, she told me to curtail my usual over-reaction—which I firmly denied—and to bring myself and something of Ivan's to her.

The sky kept its grayish look as we parked and went inside. Grey took up her usual perch by the fireplace in the family room. Ina kept a huge dog mattress there just for her.

Wait…wolf mattress. I could tell she hated the term dog.

Books lay strewn across Ina's long formal dining room table. Her table wasn't as rustic as mine. Kyle picked up the first one, did a double take and held it out to her. "What language is this?"

"Sanskrit. Don't worry. What I want to show you isn't in those books."

"Show us?" I clasped my hands behind my back as I took in the plethora of the printed word. "I dragged Kyle here because you said you would tell me about the Hammer."

"Yeah," Kyle spoke up after he returned the illegible book to the table. "Because that's some serious hooey if what Sam told me is true. I mean, I always thought that book was a joke?"

Ina looked up from the book she was reading, her glasses perched low on her nose. "The one you've seen is a joke, of a sort. We view it in this century that way because we know better. But then? Magicians were convinced that Witches were their bane and needed to be put down."

"I thought the book was created by some German priest named Heinrich Krammer?" I said.

"Oh it was. And Krammer was a Ceremonial Magician. Why do you think he really got expelled from Innsbruck?" Ina took her glasses off her face. "Gather round kiddies, cause mama's gonna take you to task."

I chuckled as I pulled out a chair and Kyle took the one opposite me at the table.

"Krammer wasn't any kind of big wig or important person in either circle, church or Magician. But what he did hate was Witches. When he brought the idea of writing down what his group had learned about Arcane Magic, knowing it had adverse effects on Witches and Magicians who used it, the Head Master of his order, as well as the bishop of Innsbrook, booted him. Now, Krammer had followers. You know the kind…they want to blame anything they don't understand for their troubles on others. These followers were made up of both

Ceremonial and Ecclesiastical scholars. Choice members of over a dozen Ceremonial groups in the world, especially in Europe, copied—in other words, stole—spells from their leader's Grimoires and gave them to Krammer in the hope of creating a master plan to rid the world of Witches."

I glanced at Kyle, whose mouth hung open. I reached across the table and tapped his chin. "Flies, dude."

He glared at me before he put his hands on the table. "You're saying all that stuff in the Hammer is real?"

"Yes, but not the one you've read. Krammer was smart when he wrote the book using an old code once used by a Ceremonial group known as The Hidden Order. Yeah. I know. Original, right?" Ina smiled as she started picking through books and pulled out a large, thin one. I guessed it was around twenty inches by twelve, about the size of a standard children's picture book. She put her glasses back on and opened the book, spinning it around for us to see. "This book, which is a reprint of one of the Order's books, has this same code worked into the words."

"Code?" I stared at the non-paragraphed type, in a language I didn't know, until my eyes crossed.

"It's not a code like say…Enigma…but more of a magical code. Now…" She set the book down, opened to the page and bent over to retrieve a rectangular black box. When she opened it, I saw my mother's athame. Ina held a finger up to silence the building protests on my lips. "No talking. You've going to have to watch."

I narrowed my eyes and was sort of aware of Kyle looking at me. I hadn't shared what I learned about my mom's athame with him yet, but honestly, I hadn't had a real moment alone when I wasn't worrying myself on something else.

Ina picked up the athame by the hilt with her left hand, held the book up for Kyle and I to see, then starting from the top, moved the blade over the left hand page.

At first nothing happened.

And then…

"Lord and Lady!" Kyle yelled. "The words are moving."

He was right. But I wouldn't have said they were moving, they were more like exchanging space. The words we knew moved from the surface of the page by sinking in, and new words took their place. But because it wasn't English, I didn't know if they said something different. "The spell is an Arcane spell. And it's not something Magicians use anymore because well...we all know what happens when we use that type of magic." She put the athame back in the box and held the book up for us to see. "Now you see the real writing in the book. The original Hammer works the same way. An object infused with an Arcane translation spell has to be passed over it."

Kyle sat back, obviously impressed.

I pointed at the box. "So you're saying...my mom's athame was infused. The fact that thing is tainted with Arcane isn't an accident."

"No, Sam. It's not. Your mother did that so she could use an Arcane spell to banish something a long...long time ago." Ina closed the book and then opened it. The spell was broken and the words were normal again.

"Did it work?"

"Did what work?"

"Mom's spell to banish? You're telling me my mother actually used Arcane."

"Yes, she did."

"So what happened?"

Ina stared at me. "She died."

I felt as if cold water had been poured over my shoulders from that two-word sentence. What I knew was she died in the line of duty. I visited her grave the entire time I lived with dad in Picayune. I respected the badge and the danger she put herself into protecting and serving.

Now Inamorata was telling me my mom's death was caused by Arcane Magic?

"Sam, I see the questions brewing and they're just going to have to wait for now. You hear me?"

I did hear her but I wasn't going to give her the satisfaction of a response. Irritation and I just didn't get along.

"Good. Now," she looked between the two of us. "I'm sure

you both know by now that the book was reportedly stolen by the Magicians and has been kept in hiding ever since?"

I nodded. I knew this because Crwys told me. Kyle…

"Kyle, ever wondered what the contention was between Magicians and Witches?"

"I thought it was as benign as the difference between Baptist and Methodist. One sprinkled and one dunked," he smiled. "Witches invite, Magicians command."

"Well yeah, that's one difference between the two. In fact it's one of the major differences. But what I'm talking about is the true root of the feud. And it all began with the Malleus Maleficarum. Some time after the hangings in Salem, the Witch Finder's original copy—the one specifically written by Krammer—was stolen. The Magicians blamed the Witches, and the Witches blamed the Magicians."

"How did the Witches blame them?" Kyle asked.

"They said the Magicians were making it all up to justify their attacks on Witches. But eventually the arguments died down and the original book became a thing of legend in a way. Detective Holliard shared a little Elder knowledge with Sam earlier this evening."

Kyle looked from Ina to me. "Crwys had Elder knowledge? What the hell is he?"

"He's not a Witch," I said in a firm tone.

"No. He's not. He's far older than that," a smile played on Ina's lips. "Kyle, this original is in the hands of the Witches and has remained so for nearly three hundred years. To keep it hidden, it's been held in safety by every High Witch in the world. They take turns protecting it."

"You mean they pass it around like a hot potato?"

"That's the general idea. Yes."

I watched Kyle's face as he put everything together, just as I had in front of Crwys.

"Sam…did Higgins have the book?"

"We're on the same page, Kyle. Only another Elder would know that for sure. But it does make more sense if Higgins was an actual target with the Changelings than just a random victim."

"And it explains why my aunt's involving herself like this," Kyle pushed his chair back, scraping it along the hardwood floor. "Medbh's insisting there's a woman after her. Someone the old Faerie's afraid of. This woman has used and is using Faerie Magic, Arcane Magic, to kill a dozen people just to get Medbh's attention, almost as if to heighten the terror for the old gal. Honestly Sam, if that crazy head is afraid of something, then I know I'm going to be terrified of it."

"Well," I began. "It's useless trying to figure out which of Medbh's countless enemies it could be and she's not talking. So let's assume she's taunting Medbh for something, probably revenge if she wants the old Queen dead. And I'm assuming this book has Arcane Magic in it that could easily destroy Medbh."

Ina sat back down. "Oh I'm sure it does. And it wouldn't be an easy death. This book wasn't created to make joy. It was created for fear."

Grey appeared at my side and rested her head in my lap. I stroked her neck and rubbed on the top of her head between her ears. "You talk about this book like it's alive."

"Sam, anytime you combine so many of something with similar energy together, things with similar focus, a gestalt forms, just like when we cut the Circle. That book has been in that form and shape for over three hundred years. Trust me…it has a personality of its own, and it's not a nice one. Even when the High Witches keep it, they never touch it. It's kept wrapped inside a delicate weave of dragon's wings to protect those around it so it can't influence their thoughts."

I stared at her. "Dragon's wings?"

Kyle spoke up. "You make it sound like this book is an accessory to the Ring of Power. Sweet Lady…do we need to find it and throw it into Mount Doom?"

I almost chuckled at that, but the reference to Ivan's favorite movies sobered me considerably as I sat forward. Grey rested beside my chair with a thud. "This isn't finding Ivan. My assumption was that Arden broke in and kidnapped him."

"Which is just stupid," Kyle said.

"And he's right, Sam. That's not Arden Vervain's style. You've got to let go of the idea she's your enemy. Move to the next possibility."

"Based on this new information and a clearer head…" I tapped my nail on the cover of a book. "I think the one Medbh's afraid of broke in with the intent of taking Medbh. But when they couldn't get to her, they took Ivan." Aw…damn. If I thought about it that way, then the only reason they'd have taken him was to use him as a bargaining piece.

I pulled my phone from my back pocket. No messages. No calls. Ivan had been gone two hours.

"Samantha," Ina leaned forward and put her hand on the book in front of me. "Go back and talk to Medbh. *Talk* to her. Don't threaten. And," she held up a finger before she stood and left the room.

Kyle put his hands on his thighs and stood. "I'll go crank the Jeep."

"Yeah. Take Grey with you."

Ina returned after he and Grey went outside. She handed me a flat wooden box. It was six by six. "The wood is rowan wood, which should immediately calm her. But I think she'll be more easily swayed if you give this to her."

Inside was a silver herringbone chain, maybe a half inch in width. The lights caught the silver and spilled radiance on the lid's interior. But what caught my eye was the sparkling blue topaz jewel set in the center of the herringbone chain. "Where…"

"It belonged to my great aunt. I've had it for over thirty years. She willed it to me."

"Oh…no. Ina I can't take this and offer it to Medbh. Mostly because I think Faeries react to silver the same way they react to iron, right?"

"No. That's just iron. Silver is sometimes deadly to a particular type of Vampire and it's definitely not comfortable for a Lycan."

I shook my head. "Still…Medbh isn't worth giving up something so nice for."

"Maybe not, but Ivan is." She knelt beside me and put her hand on my shoulder. This close she smelled of jasmine and sage. "What makes us different than the Faeries, than any of the creatures of *Alfheim*, is our value of life. It's something they don't have. They can't understand. This little bauble has sat in my chest for as long as I've had it. I never wear it, and I never will. Take it. Use it. You can't move forward until you know what it is you're moving against. You're shooting in the dark here, Sammie."

I closed the box and stood. She stood with me. When I hugged her, I squeezed as tight as I dared. "I love you, Ina."

"I love you. Just as I loved your mother." She pulled back and tucked a strand of my unruly hair behind my ear. "Now go. Find out who is behind it, and once you have that, you'll know what step to take next."

FOURTEEN

Ina's suggestion worked a miracle.

Not only did Medbh's entire demeanor shift when I put the box next to her, her voice changed back to Aunt B and she adopted a southern accent. A *bad*…southern accent. I'm sorry…but we don't sound like that.

Something else I noticed as Kyle and I pulled up stools to talk to Medbh. The chips, scars and cracks on the head were less noticeable. Were they actually healing?

"Medbh," I began as I put my hand on the box. "I need you to tell me everything about this person that's after you. The one controlling the Changelings. And if you tell me, you can have what's in the box and I'll do my best to protect you."

She didn't answer at first. But when she did, her voice sounded as if it were filled with emotion. :*You'd do that…for me?*:

"Yes, I would. You're under my care and so far my wards protected you. But I have to protect Ivan too, and I need you to tell me everything. Otherwise I can't fight them."

The head didn't move for several seconds, and then it rocked just a bit to face me. I reached out and pulled the incense stick from its nose. And to my astonishment, the hole closed up.

"You know," Kyle said as he leaned in close to me. "Rowan wood has healing properties to it."

:*Yes, it does. Just having the box next to me is enough. Show me what's inside?*:

"Tell me what you know. Please, Medbh."

:Fourteen years ago, a woman summoned me using a very old, tried and true spell. It'd been decades since anyone had used our magic, other than ourselves. She told me her name was Dionysus.:

Kyle held up his hands. "Whoa…this *woman* said her name was Dionysus? You mean like the Greek God?"

:Yes.:

"That's messed up. Was she human?"

:She had been human once. But I sensed that was a long time ago.:

I suddenly had a thought. And I didn't like it. "Medbh, when you said the shop filled with witchy ninjas…they weren't Ghouls, were they?"

:Yes.:

Damn.

"Dionysus is a Vampire," Kyle rubbed his face. "Great. That makes her, him, harder to find. What is with these demons and their power trip names?"

"Eh, they all have them," I said. "But they're not harder to detect. Remember, I can sense Vampires."

Medbh laughed. *:You can sense what we call the white Vampires. Revenants. Those demons join with humans to share a body. But Dionysus doesn't share, she takes.:*

The hairs along my neck stood on end. "You mean there's no dual possession."

:None. There are those demons like Dionysus who take hold of a human body without permission. They do not give the human the option of inviting them in. They ride the human souls inside, use them as their mini-throne to torture and bind the body to do their will. These are the ones we call Leviathans.:

Great. Revenants and Leviathans. I was going to need to write this shit down.

I blew air out between my lips. "What did Dionysus want?"

:She wanted me to get rid of a Witch. This Witch had learned all her secrets, even her tells. Everywhere Dionysus turned, the Witch was there:

"Why you? Why not just get rid of the Witch herself?" Kyle asked. "She's a Vampire. Vampires can kill Witches."

:Not this Witch. Dionysus had tried three times to kill the Witch, and each time the Witch survived. Then she learned the Witch was using Arcane Magic to keep one step ahead of Dionysus. That's when she turned to me.:

I looked around the floor and into the other room. Where was Grey?

"And?" Kyle prompted.

:She struck a deal with me. I would remove this Witch from the world, and she would give me something in return.:

The thought of a Vampire making a deal with a Faerie surprised me. "Dionysus must've been desperate. What did she give you?"

During the conversation I noticed ongoing improvements in the condition of the ceramic head. The chips and dings were almost non-existent, and the paint was less faded.

:She offered me her soul.:

I choked. Kyle nearly fell off his stool. "Medbh—Faeries can't steal souls. That's ridiculous."

:Not from a human directly. But we can remove the soul from a Vampire. So she offered up the soul of the body she possessed.:

Kyle tilted his head to his right shoulder. "What's the catch? Deals with your kind don't always work—strike that—they *never* work in favor of the other party."

:Vampires have to have the human soul to keep them anchored in the body. That applies to both Revenant and Leviathan. In order for Dionysus to keep the body I had to fuse her to the framework.:

"What does that mean?" Kyle looked at me.

I stared at Medbh. "It means she fused Dionysus to the skeleton of her host. Which, if I remember the consequences of this little trick, makes it impossible for the demon to leave the body and find a new one."

:Precisely!: Medbh sounded almost festive. *:I did my part, but once I came for my price, Dionysus decided she didn't want to finish the deal. Much like you not finishing your agreement with Brendi.:*

I let that little jab slide. Mostly because she was right.

:I called a Hunt, we took Dionysus and I took the soul.:

"What did you do with it?" I asked.

:*Returned it to the Well of Souls. I keep my promises.*: The head tilted a little. :*Most of the time. Dionysus has been looking for me ever since, and until eight or so months ago I was safe in* Alfheim.:

"Now you're vulnerable."

:*Yes. And she knows it. She knows where I am. Using those Changelings was her way of showing me she could master Arcane Faerie Magic. But I doubt she has a means to actually destroy me.*:

"What happens if she destroys you?" Kyle asked.

:*The spell would be broken and she would be ejected from the body. She would need a host ready and waiting for her or her own essence will be called back to the Well. It's what happens to body snatchers. But she doesn't have that kind of power. Creating and controlling Changelings is child's play compared to the kind of power she'll need to destroy me.*:

"Medbh, I hate to be the bearer of seriously 'effed up news, but we think she does have the means, or she's at least figured out what means she needs."

:*That made no sense.*:

Kyle held up his hand, signaling to me that he wanted to deliver the news. "Malleus Maleficarum."

The reaction was instantaneous. The head started vibrating and spinning a little. Sort of looked like it was searching the room for ghosts. :*No. You can't let her get hold of that book. That thing has magic in it that could literally destroy the world.*:

"We think that's why one of the Changelings took out Mr. Higgins. He was the local High Witch and the one we think was in possession of this original tome." I rubbed at my chin and pulled my phone out to check the time.

:*If she had it, I'd be dead already. Did this Higgins keep the book in his home?*:

"I don't know." I was a little remiss that I hadn't asked Ina if she knew the answer to that. "Normally, I'd ask Ivan to check and see if he could find anything about break-ins." But Ivan wasn't there. "Medbh, if Dionysus was in my store today, why did she take Ivan? It's been hours and I haven't gotten a phone call, a text message—nothing. I figured she'd ransom him for you."

:He fought. Hard. I think he fascinated her because she realized he could see Arcane.:

Aw damn. "Crap. How did she figure that out?"

:She's not like other Vampires. Remember, she's a Leviathan. They're different, and they're stronger. She can hear other's thoughts, so I'm sure she figured out his nature pretty fast.:

But why take him if no ransom demands? Unless she planned on using Ivan's power to her advantage. He could see Arcane as well as smell it. If they wanted to find that damn book in Higgins's house, having an Arcane detector would be an advantage. But, being Arcane herself, wouldn't she be able to see it? Sense it? I don't know…feel it?

"Medbh," Kyle said as he shifted on the stool. "What is the worst thing Dionysus would do with Ivan? Or, I hate to say it, *to* Ivan?"

:The worst would be relative to what Ivan finds most distasteful. If she is able to find that book and free herself, she could use him as her new vessel. Ride him like a magic pony, to put it bluntly. Think about a Leviathan possessing Ivan's sort of magic?:

"Eh," I said with a shrug. "We already have a million crazy, megalomaniacal bitches loose on the web. What's one more? What we need to do is get that book."

"And do what?" Kyle stood up and moved the stool out of his way. "We can't use it. And to quote Gandalf, I won't touch it."

I slipped off my stool as well. "We just need to stop Dionysus from using it." I made a face at Kyle. "Is it me, or does it seem weird saying Dionysus?"

"It's weird, especially since the image I had in my head was of a hot young guy in a toga," he pointed to the box. "You giving her the sparkly?"

"Yeah." I put my hands on the box. It was warm and instantly made me feel…better. Rowan wood. "Medbh, what happened to the Witch? The one Dionysus wanted dead?"

:I'm not sure. I grabbed a lot of Witches back then. Kinda got on this kick about making mutts.:

I smirked. "You mean like Brendi Ross?"

Medbh made a rude noise. Brendi was the reason the old queen was bodiless. :*Yeah. Like that. I'm pretty sure she's dead, though. Not many Witches survived the transformation.*:

"Transformation?"

:*Into hunting wolves…so, what's in the box?*:

Kyle stepped up. "What was the Witch's name? Maybe we can look her up and that could help with finding out more about Dionysus, and about whatever body she's riding like a pony now?"

Medbh bounced. :*What's in the box?*:

"Answer his question," I said.

If a ceramic head could make a frustrated tweenager noise, Medbh could. And she did. :*Fine. Her name was Elizabeth something…*:

I narrowed my eyes. "Elizabeth?" My mom's name had been Elizabeth. It was my middle name.

:*Lemme see what's in the box and I'll tell you the rest!*:

"Tell me *before*."

She didn't budge.

"Fine." I opened the box to expose the shiny silver necklace and jewel. "Tell me."

:*Hawthor—*:

Something bright and mind-achingly loud flashed out of that box. My natural defenses kicked in as pentagrams of blue, yellow, green and red sprang up around Medbh and the box, only I couldn't see either the head or the box through the blinding light. The pentagrams spun deosil, then widdershins, then deosil (clockwise, counter-clockwise, clockwise), as they worked to contain whatever magic exploded out at that moment.

I heard a voice screaming in the chaos and put my hands over my ears. It sounded like a thousand freight trains barreling through the shop and into the basement and then—

Silence.

When it was over, I was crouched on the ground with Kyle beside me. We both had our hands up, and around us pulsed a white mist. I poked at it and it popped like a bubble. "You do that?"

Kyle sniffed. "Yeah. I made a sachet last night for protection."

"It worked." I stood on shaky knees and he put his hand out as he stood.

"I'm thinking…silver and Faeries is bad," Kyle said as he moved past me to the table where Medbh and the box rested.

I gasped when I saw the head. It was completely white. No paint. No holes. Not even a ding. It looked like someone had covered it in a shiny coat of white paint. The necklace remained in the box, the topaz twinkling under the single bulb in the basement. The Elemental pentagrams still spun like gears in the air before I dismissed them.

"Medbh?"

No answer. Not even a hint of her.

"No…no, no, no, no…" This wasn't happening. I grabbed her up with both of my hands and shook her. "Don't you disappear on me. You said Hawthorne. I heard you say Hawthorne. Did you mean Elizabeth Hawthorne? You took a Witch with that name—"

"Hey, calm down," Kyle said as he put a hand on my shoulder and quickly took the featureless head from my hands. "Stop it."

"Give that back to me." I reached out for Medbh's head, but Kyle held it out of my reach like a bully taunting a smaller kid with their prize.

"Sam, you need to calm down. Take a deep breath. And let go of my arm. Now step over there," he lowered the head and looked at it. "I don't think she's in here anymore."

"Because of the necklace?" I picked the necklace out of the box and held it up. It didn't feel any different. Just silver. And topaz.

"The silver. I think we just don't know enough about real Faerie lore."

"Did…did it kill her?" I dropped the necklace back into the box and put my hand on the head in Kyle's grasp. "Medbh. Please…don't stop now. Please…did you mean my mother? Elizabeth Hawthorne?"

Deafening silence.

"This can't be right, can it? I thought your mom died while doing cop stuff. In the line of duty."

I nodded as I gently took the head from his hands. "Yeah. That's what I was told. By my dad. By Ina. By everyone." I set the head back on the table and shut the box. "I don't…I don't know what to think."

My phone rang. I pulled it out and didn't recognize the number. "Hello?"

"Miss Hawthorne?"

"Yes?" I put the head back in the safe and closed it.

"This is Doctor Redmond over at Tulane. I spoke with Rose Matisse's brother last night. You were with him. A Mr. Robin Tremere?"

I shut the box and picked it up as I walked to the basement steps. "Yes. What's wrong?"

"I hate to be the bearer of bad news. Rose passed away an hour ago and her brother has collapsed. He's in ICU and he listed you as a contact person."

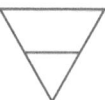

FIFTEEN

With two mysterious deaths within twenty-four hours and now Robin exhibiting the same symptoms, the hospital wasn't taking any chances. What if this was contagious and someone else contracted it? Just mention the word lawsuit and the administrators sat up to take note.

The nurses dressed me in booties and the full paper jumpsuit before they let me in ICU. I pulled my hair into a paper cap and had trouble with my trembling hands when I put on the mask.

I had one nurse look at me funny and asked if I was in the hospital with Mr. Tremere the night before. I knew where she was going with that line of thought and instantly pushed a bit of Spirit her way, giving her a nice high and a very erratic memory.

The last thing I needed was to get caught up in some useless quarantine.

I shuffled closer to Robin, almost afraid to look at him. I had images of sores eating his flesh and blood coming from his nose. So when he turned his head to look at me, I wasn't prepared.

He looked like Robin, just as beautiful as ever, but pale. Shadows in his face made him look thin and his skin had a greenish tinge to it. My usual rein over my magic vanished as my hand touched his. The *dex* spell launched and I watched the banishing pentagrams search his entire body. Even they couldn't give me what I needed to know.

An antidote.

I could smell the Arcane oozing from his pours through my

107

mask. Apparently Ina's salve hadn't helped at all. Robin's condition was steadily worsening. The doctors didn't think he'd survive past dawn.

He put a hand to my cheek and I closed my eyes. "Oh baby. It's going to be okay. You'll see."

Robin's voice was so light and airy, I wondered if he knew his sister had died. If he didn't, I decided I wasn't going to be the one to give him the bad news. I put my gloved hands on his and kissed his wrist through the paper material. "I know. I can't stay. I just wanted to see you. Tell you I love you."

"I love you." He coughed. Blood appeared on his lip and I immediately grabbed tissues out of the box by the bed and dabbed at it. "Sorry…" he said. "That keeps happening. But I can't imagine what it is I ate to make it happen. I keep telling them to check for appendicitis."

"I doubt that's it, baby." I slipped the tissue under my sleeve. "I have to go do a few things. One of the boys is in trouble."

"I bet it's Kyle."

"No. It's Ivan. But I'll be back tonight, okay? As soon as I can."

The smile he gave me was so full of warmth I blinked back the burning behind my eyes. No one had survived this. I couldn't get that thought out of my head.

He patted my hand. "You go do your thing, okay? I'll be here waiting for you."

I nodded but nothing was stopping the waterworks. I was an emotional mess. I kissed his forehead. He squeezed my hand.

I tore off the paper suit as I left ICU. I didn't sign out even as the nurse called out my name. I threw everything into the proper receptacle and the tissue fell out and onto the floor. My life came spinning into sharp focus as I stood there, transfixed by the blood.

All my life I'd been a good girl. I'd done what I was told to do. I made good grades. I took care of the house for dad. And I made Aunt Ina proud with my mastery of my Gift. And all that time, was it possible they had lied to me about my mother? I didn't have a clear memory of the night she died, other than I had been worried about a play, but I never went to that play because I had a funeral.

I knew so little about my mom, other than she was a Witch, and a detective, and she was good at both vocations. Ina reassured me, though my dad never mentioned the magic side of things. And Ina thought it best to keep those things out of his sight. Was it because he knew the truth of how she died?

Was it because he knew she'd been taken by a Faerie Queen? During a Hunt?

Somehow I didn't think that was possible. Not my dad. I doubted he knew anything beyond what he told me.

But what about Ina? There had been a coven once. Or so she said. But my mom's death disheartened everyone and it closed. But she stayed with me through it all.

Ina had to know the truth.

There were too many things I needed to do. I needed those answers about my mom, but I needed to find Ivan first. I needed that book. If I had that book I could get the truth from Dionysus, the one who arranged the death or the disappearance of my mom.

I had to stop and rethink that. Disappearance didn't seem right. I had to believe that if my mom were still alive, she'd have tried to find me somehow. Maybe…maybe my aunt had gone along with the story to make life easier for me.

"Miss?"

The voice to my left made me jump and I looked into the dark eyes of a woman in teddy bear scrubs. "Y-Yes?"

"Are you okay? Should I call someone?"

"No. I'm fine." I bent down and picked up the tissue. "Just…been a really rough day."

"Oh, I'm in touch with that emotion, child. You take care out there."

I was already heading to the elevator as I stuffed the tissue into my jeans pocket.

A long black limousine pulled into the hospital's drive as I stepped outside. I turned to the left, headed in the direction of my Jeep as the front passenger door opened and a man in a nice black suit stepped out. "Miss Hawthorne?"

Wasn't expecting that, so I half turned and gave him a questioning look. "Who wants to know?"

The man flashed me a million dollar smile and opened the rear passenger door. "My employer. Would you please step inside?"

Now, I'm not in the habit of getting into strange cars. Even strange limos. And I didn't know anyone who drove around New Orleans in a limo. One would expect Arden Vervain to afford such luxuries, but she liked driving herself places, according to her nephew.

I am in the habit of listening to my internal alarms. And those suckers were popping off one after the other. I summoned my *dex* to see what was in the limo. Three, two, one and the man with the smile was human, but the spell couldn't penetrate the vehicle. That meant whoever was inside didn't want to be discovered or seen until they were ready.

"Miss Hawthorne," Mr. Smile said in a very low and calming tone. "My employer has instructed me to tell you that if you don't get in the car, it's unlikely you will see your friend Mr. Westerfield alive again."

Now he had my attention, and my wrath. I thinned my lips, straightened my shoulders and cautiously stepped into the back of the limo. Those inside had the element of sight since my eyes had to adjust to the dim lighting as I slid into a seat facing the rear and Mr. Smile closed the door.

Let's just say when I got a good look at my host, my jaw dragged the pavement as the limo pulled away from the hospital. "Arwen?"

It was her, but she didn't look like the meek little student I'd met the night before. She was decked out in a little black leather outfit and matching boots. Her hair was pulled back in a tight ponytail and her make up had gone from cubicle daytime to street corner nighttime. Her jewelry, all gold in tones, had a slight Egyptian motif to it. "The name's Dio, but I do prefer to be called Arwen."

Dionysus.

Fucking. Hell. The damn Leviathan had been under mine and Ina's noses the whole time. I reacted on instinct with the intent of summoning the banishing spell and getting rid of this evil piece of shit once and for all.

Intent being the key word.

I couldn't move. Too late, I realized I was paralyzed from the neck down as a cold, seeping ice moved from my toes up to my chin.

Arwen laughed. "It's a nice little spell, don't you think? Something I picked up from a former Witch Finder. Little Dianic beast of a man. He liked to lure young Witches into his car and paralyze them before he took them back to his barn and did all kinds of terrible things to them."

I glared at her. "Where is Ivan?"

"He's alive, if that's what you want to know. I haven't done any permanent damage to him. Though he did put up one hell of a fight at your little shop." She leaned forward, her hands clasped. Her nails were painted a rich, deep red. "That's a very interesting Gift he has, don't you think? Not only can he surf the web with no computer, magnetic fields don't disrupt his spells and he can actually see Arcane Magic. Such a rare little find."

"You will *not* use him." Wow. That sounded so…tough. Rawr. Gimme a bone to gnaw.

Arwen leaned back in her seat and waved her hand. "Already did. And I was very disappointed. I assume you know who I am and how you and I are connected?"

I didn't know the whole story and the truth was apparently on my face.

"Oh, well let me bring you up to speed so we can talk about working together. Your mother was after me. Had been…after me for years. She was good at what she did, which was tracking down demons like us. See," she pointed to her chest. "I'm not like those soft Vampires you've met, my brothers and sisters, who prefer to play footsies with their hosts. I prefer domination, and obedience, and I get it. Except with your damn mother."

My jaw tightened as I watched her. I could move my head, look around, talk and breathe, but not much of anything else. My Elements swirled around me, bashing and trying to slash their way out of whatever spell this was. The smell of Arcane was sickening.

"So I went to the Faerie Queen and made a deal."

"You asked Medbh to take my mother and you offered up the soul of that body."

"Offered?" Arwen squinted at me and put her hands to her sides on the leather seat as the limo made a wide right turn. "Offered? Oh no...*no*. That bitch didn't tell me what she wanted until she tried to take it. She showed me what she did to your mother before she demanded her payment."

I swallowed. I wanted to ask her what. I wanted to know. And then again, I didn't want to, because that would mean knowing if she suffered. My memories of my mother were vague. I couldn't remember her face, or the color of her hair or how tall she was. But I could remember things about her. Her laugh. I'll always remember her laugh. And her smell. She had the best smell in the world. It was the smell of home.

"That fucking Faerie chased me all over the city to take this soul. But when I found out what she intended to do to me, I managed to escape once. Then she caught me nearly a month after your mother's alleged death. That bitch fused me," she lifted her hand and beat at her chest. "*Me*, to this goddamn carcass. I'm a God, little Witch. I am a fucking force of nature. And that wingless wonder locked me into a physical body, preventing me from continuing *my* right of survival."

It grated my nerves listening to her. She had no care about the soul she traded off, though the real Arwen was probably better off being returned to the Well, if what Medbh said was true. But what really started growing, as a toxic realization, inside my mind was I was facing my mother's killer. This vain, selfish creature hired someone to kill my mother just because she was bothering it.

"And now you want to destroy Medbh so you can get out of that body and into another one."

She smiled. It made me feel oily. "Exactly. But in order to destroy Medbh, I need the Malleus Maleficarum, which I know you are familiar with thanks to Inamorata. I thought that bald headed bore of a High Witch had it. But when he refused to give it to me, I made sure his niece ripped him a new one."

Holy hell...that kid had been Higgins' niece? I tried wiggling my finger. Nothing. Whatever spell this was, it was good. But now I was shivering with the cold.

"I took your little Cyber Witch to Higgins's house today because I was sure the damn book was there. Nothing. But what I did discover was Arden Vervain was in the house last night. Before me. I'm more than sure she has it. Which brings us to the reason I wanted to talk to you."

So Arden had the book? *Sweet Lady…I hope like hell she didn't try and use it.* Having something that evil influencing Arden Vervain?

Goddess help us all.

Figuring out what Arwen wanted wasn't hard. "You want me to get the book from Arden. I give it to you and you'll give me Ivan back."

"I knew you were smart. Smarter than your mother was."

I am going to kill you. This was the only thought in my head as Arwen laid out her little plan to get the book. I half paid attention. My imagination was full of all the different ways I planned on ending this bitch's life. Crwys had said this book had an exorcism spell inside of it. Something that would remove the demon from its host. Exactly how painful would it be for Dionysus to be physically removed from a body she was fused into?

The fact I enjoyed the thought scared me.

"Do we have an agreement, Miss Hawthorne?"

I refocused on her. "You let Ivan go. Now."

"That's not going to happen until I have the book."

I might have been stuck where I was, unable to gesticulate wildly like I so wanted to do, but that wasn't going to stop me from playing what cards I had. "And you're not getting that book until I have Ivan back with me. The way I see it, the only reason you're talking to me is because you can't get into Arden Vervain's home. And I'm willing to bet you tried before you ever even considered hunting me down. I can't see Arcane essence, or whatever it is. Ivan can. I am going to need him to see it in her house. Arden's smart. She's probably covered it in spells. How else am I going to find it?"

"But if you have Ivan, I don't have leverage."

"Yes you do," I licked my lips. "You can cure Robin Tremere. A victim of one the Changelings. The creator of the Changeling sets the venom. That would be you. You have the cure."

Arwen's brow arched high on her forehead. "He's important to you?"

I swallowed. This was a lot more information than I wanted to give her, but if I had my way at the end of this it wouldn't matter.

Because I was going to *kill* her. Not banish.

Kill.

Arwen looked as if she were considering this as she looked out the window, a far away look in her eyes. A sly smile pulled at her lips before she looked back at me. "You have a deal. Ivan will be delivered to you shortly. You have until midnight to retrieve the book."

The limo came to a stop and suddenly I could move. I hadn't realized how tense I was until I nearly fell out of the seat. The door opened and Mr. Smile was there with his hand.

I climbed out on wobbly knees in front of my store. Mr. Smile shut the door, bowed to me and I watched as he drove the hulking car down Bourbon Street. The fact he found my shop told me Mr. Smile, though human, could see the magical world. The sky still threatened some serious rain and my Jeep was still at the hospital. Crap.

I had just put my hand on the door handle, when the screech of tires on asphalt made me turn my head. Tourists and locals shouted and cursed as a black van careened around the corner of St. Philip and came barreling in my direction. I moved out of the way as it made an abrupt stop in front of me and the side door slid open.

Two women dressed like ninjas (seriously, like ninjas) stepped out as Ivan was shoved from inside. He landed on his side at my curb. I ran to him as the ninjas got back in the van and the vehicle sped away with the same lack of grace it arrived in.

Ivan was curled up in a ball, his knees drawn into his chest. "Sam…" He said in a tight voice. "I really have to pee."

SIXTEEN

I helped Ivan stand and he leaned heavily on my shoulder. I didn't get a good look at him until we were inside the shop. The place had been cleaned up and what product wasn't damaged, neatly rearranged on new tables and shelves. I didn't know what had happened in here—maybe Kyle had come in and done his Hedgey Magic—but I would deal with it later.

The store bathrooms were decent, but mine was better. Grey greeted me as we came up the stairs from the shop entrance.

My apartment consisted of five rooms. It was as wide and as long as the building itself and the owners before me had made use of every inch of space. The steps came into the main room. One wall consisted of a set of French doors that led out onto the building length balcony overlooking Bourbon Street. I had a flat screen on the opposite wall with an Ikea couch facing it. Matching chairs on either side flanked one of my dad's old coffee tables. On the right was the kitchen and dining area. It wasn't a big kitchen, but it was as modern as I could afford for the age of the building. On the left were the two bedrooms and a single bathroom. The balcony and the clawfoot tub were two selling points for me when it came to keeping the apartment for myself and not renting it out. It was more expensive this way, but I always managed to make it work.

Managed was the right word. I knew once I got through the present crisis, the next would be whether or not I could convince the insurance to fix that window. Ugh…not to mention the product I'd lost during Arwen's little redecoration inside the store.

115

Ivan ran into the bathroom and slammed the door. But what I heard wasn't the norm—it sounded like he was throwing up. And I knew just the tea for nausea, thanks to Kyle. I started the electric kettle and placed a bag of my partner's special brew into two mugs. Wouldn't hurt if *I* had some of the tea, given the news and revelations I'd just been subjected to.

I was on the couch with the tea service on the coffee table when Ivan emerged. He looked…

My jaw dropped when I finally saw his face. His left cheek and eye were swollen and his lower lip had a nasty cut on it. His clothes were ripped and torn and I spotted bruises on his exposed wrists. He clutched his chest in an odd way when he sat down next to me. I turned and scooted closer. "Lean to me," I said with my hands out.

"No," he said as he shook his head. "You can't heal me yet."

"Like hell." I clapped my hands together once, and then slowly started pulling them apart to create the healing matrix I was going to need to—

His touch on my wrist disrupted my concentration and the forming yellow ball of light evaporated. "Not yet. I've got something to tell you, and show you, and then…if you still want to…I'll agree to it."

"If I still want to?" I searched his exotic face. "What…what the hell happened, Ivan?"

"First thing is I know who's behind it all. It's that crazy blond from Ina's group. The one that called herself Arwen—"

"Yeah, I know. She and I had a little chat. Tell me what happened."

"Kyle had just left when the store filled with…the best way to put it is tall, leggy female ninjas. I know how crazy it sounds, but that's what I saw. And given they were all female they caught me by surprise. They moved fast."

I smiled at him and tucked a strand or two of that wild hair of his behind his ear. Two of his hoops were gone and the holes ripped open. "I suspected they were Ghouls. Dionysus's Ghouls."

He smiled at me. "That's exactly what they were. Only I didn't know that at the time. My magic's more defensive than offensive so I wasn't sure how to attack them and when it came to defending—they weren't using anything electronic. It was like they already knew my weakness."

I was betting they did. How—I wasn't clear on that yet. Ina's statement that Dionysus wasn't an ordinary Vampire but a Leviathan still wasn't sinking in. "Go on."

"The women started hitting and punching and generally beat the crap out of me. I felt like I was on the playground again and getting pummeled for my lunch money." He made a face. He had a really nice face, when it wasn't bruised. "I could see those little red worms. They were everywhere. They were on the women, and crawling all over their bodies. In their mouths and their eyes. I don't know how but Arwen knew I could see Arcane Magic. I didn't say this and I didn't tell her, but she threatened to kill you and Kyle if I didn't show her where the book was. No one believed me when I told them I didn't know what they were talking about.

"They drove me to that store owner's house. Mr. Higgins? The guy lived in a mansion, Sam. It was huge. And it had all kinds of secret passageways and magical traps. He also had some serious electronic surveillance. But the women had me shut it down and erase any recordings."

"Arwen said you didn't find the book." There was something off about him—I couldn't put my finger on it, but it had something to do with the way I was seeing him. His face or his hands— "Ivan, you're swollen. I mean you're swollen besides the punches."

He nodded. "Yeah. I'll show you why in two seconds. Truth was I did find the book. It was in Higgins's bedroom, just lying on his bed. I didn't recognize it at first because it was wrapped in some weird leathery stuff. But when I touched it, I could see the red stuff just under the leather. When I peeled the leather back, the book looked like it was made of those worms. I didn't know what the book was but I knew this was what they were looking for and there was no way this chick could have it so…" he looked away from me.

"Ivan? What happened?"

"The book was just wrong…I knew I couldn't let anyone know it was there…"

PHAEDRA WELDON

Oh sweet Lady. "Ivan…you didn't destroy it, did you?"

"No. I did something else." He fidgeted and then leaned forward and grabbed his tea before he said, "I…uh…I uploaded it."

I tilted my head to my right shoulder. I wasn't quite sure I'd heard that right. "You…*uploaded* it?"

"There's no other way to describe what happened. I was standing there, panicking and I just wanted the thing to disappear. So…I started wishing there was a way to hide it and suddenly all those little red worms turned green and they formed a line into my fingers."

He held his hands out to me, palms up. "I stood there with my mouth hanging open, just watching that entire book shift into code. Sam…I turned a physical object into *code*!"

My jaw hung open. We all used forms of transmutation in magic every day. I turned the Elements into entities and energies I could use. Kyle transmuted plants, herbs and symbols into forms of magic he could utilize and bend. I had watched Crwys transmute a window into sand.

So why not transmute a solid object into code?

Because it was just too far out and creepy…

But then my brain kicked in as I realized the book was real. The book was *real*! It had been material. It existed! I leaned forward and put my hands on his. "Can you download it?"

"I don't know. I've been wondering that ever since. In fact, that's all I've been thinking about. We left Higgins's house and I was tossed into the back of a van, handcuffed to a metal hook drilled into the floorboard. Then a bunch of them jumped in the van and they dumped me out here."

"So you haven't tried to download it?"

"No. I really, really want to get rid of it, you know? I feel full, heavier than I should. But because know the book's Arcane I didn't know if you'd be okay with that since all you've ever told me was to stay away from Arcane and then I actually uploaded an entire book made of the stuff—"

I put a firm hand on his cheek. He finally looked at me. "Download it now."

Ivan's smile lit up my day before he set his tea back on the coffee table. He turned around and leaned against the sofa's back. He had his hands on his knees and closed his eyes. I wondered how long it would take or what it would look like.

Nothing…and I mean *nothing* could have prepared me for what happened next.

The lights in the room flickered like they did when I turned on my printer. Ivan moved forward as he put his hands together as if in prayer. He slowly pulled his hands part and as he did, green lights flickered and moved back and forth between his fingers. He continued to pull his hands apart as the green lights formed themselves into a book.

Not a very big book, maybe the size of a hard cover. It was little more than an outline in different hues of green. The lights moved faster and Ivan bowed his head. I could see strain on his face. This was draining him again.

The green darkened and shifted to brown. The leather surface of the book hardened and took shape as the pages formed on the inside. Maybe five minutes passed since he started and he was sitting there, hands held out as a book formed and floated between them.

Abruptly the lights brightened again and the book fell into his lap. Ivan would have fallen face first off the couch if I hadn't scrambled forward and nearly stepped on Grey to get to him. He held onto me as the book slipped from his lap to the floor.

I was worried about Ivan. He was heavy against me and his breathing was ragged. "Ivan…" I felt my own magic stir, giving him a few jolts where he needed it.

His breathing evened out and he finally sat back on his own. "I don't want to do that again for a while."

"You don't have to."

Grey growled at the book on the floor. She was also on her feet, staring at it like it was going to attack her.

I gently pushed her aside and picked the book up. It was light and instantly made my fingers numb.

I let it hit the coffee table where the impact made the coffee cups jump. "That's odd. It was light in my hand but hit the table like a stack of books."

"The weight hasn't evened out yet. Just give it a second or two."

"And you've never done this before?"

"No. But I somehow know how to," he turned his expressive eyes to me. "Is this how it works? Magic, I mean. It sort of folds in on itself sometimes and then it does something bigger and different than before?"

"Yeah. This is how it works. You should have seen me the first time I healed anyone. But right now you're going to need sleep."

"I don't have a choice," he leaned in and kissed my cheek. "You can have it now. It won't transmute again. You can count on it." He stood and stumbled his way to the smaller room and closed the door.

I sat on the couch and stared at this book.

A book of Arcane Magic.

I could smell it.

It made the air acrid with its stench.

When I reached out to touch it again, Grey nudged my hand away with her nose. She was looking at me as if pleading. Every time I tried to touch the book, she pushed me away. Frustrated, I grabbed her by her collar and dragged her into my bedroom and locked the door.

She howled and barked at first, until I closed the wards around my home, instantly silencing her and everything else as I gingerly pulled away the thin, leather-like covering and opened the book.

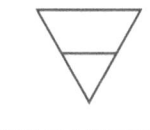

SEVENTEEN

My ringtone jolted me out of an hour of frustrated reading. It was the same damn drivel I'd read years ago. The same translation that made me throw it at the wall then made me want to chuck it out the window now. Ina had used my mom's athame to see the writing hidden under the printed copy of that book. I might have to borrow Mom's athame to read what was in this book. I slammed the book shut and shoved it under the couch before I realized there wasn't anyone else in the room but me, and whoever was calling me couldn't see what I was doing. I didn't know why I felt so guilty reading the book but I did. I think it was because it was something forbidden; something I'd always been taught was dangerous to me.

Everyone said Arcane Magic was bad. Well, how was something supposed to be bad if you couldn't *find* it?

I lifted up my hip and dug the phone out of my back pocket. "Yeah."

"It's me," Crwys said.

"I thought you weren't talking to me anymore."

He paused and I imagined he was trying to hold his temper in check. "Just come downstairs."

"Are you in my shop?"

"I'm in the back. With Levi. And if you try to banish him, I'll shoot you where you stand."

I hung up. That bastard. How did he get in with my wards up? I stood and pulled the lace curtains covering my wall of windows to the side. His Mustang was parked on the road below.

There weren't any missed messages from the hospital, so I was pretty sure whatever was bothering him wasn't about Robin. I shoved the phone into my jeans pocket, grabbed the book and headed downstairs. But before I stepped into the store, I went into the basement and hid the book in one of the boxes marked business papers. I threw up a few wards, but felt pretty confident the book wasn't as visible with the leather covering on it.

Levi was dressed in his usual suit and tie, looking as classic as ever. He offered to make me a cup of tea and I nodded. Crwys, dressed in worn jeans, boots, t-shirt and leather jacket looked less classy, but very sexy. He stood at the opposite end of the table with a folder in his hand. I looked at Levi. "What's wrong?"

"You'll see. But," he said as he held out his hand. "Keep an open mind, okay? And try not to banish me before you hear him out."

Crap. Crwys told Levi I threatened him. "You two mind telling me what this is about? Why the stoic look?"

"Sit down and take a look at the folder, okay?" He didn't look at me. Grey came down the stairs and padded up to me. I didn't know how she got out of the room…unless Ivan woke and opened the door. She didn't seem angry with me for locking her up so I ran my fingers through her thick coat as I sat in a chair and pulled the folder towards me.

The name on the tab read Elizabeth "Eliza" Rowen Hawthorne, Lt. Detective. I froze. "Why do you have a folder with my mother's name on it?"

Levi pulled the chair out at the head of the table and sat down. "We know who's behind the Changelings and it's not Medbh."

"I know. It's a demon named Dionysus," I looked at Levi. "One of your family?"

The two of them exchanged worried looks. It was Levi that changed his appearance though, as his eyes became solid black and his voice took on the dual nature of a Vampire when their demon spoke through them. Levi's demon's name was Ashur. "Yes…*he's* one of my family. A distant brother, much older than myself. I'm still fairly young by comparison. Don't worry about the he or she pronoun. It's not important. Once Dionysus learned he could take any human at any time, sex no longer mattered to him."

Crwys snorted. "Sexual partners never mattered much to him either, if I recall."

Ashur/Levi shrugged. "I forgot you knew Dio, before he stepped out on his own."

I looked from one to the other. "Can we get to the point?" The comment about Crwys knowing Dionysus wasn't lost on me. I just didn't have the time or the patience.

"Dionysus isn't like us," Ashur put his hand to his chest. "There are those in my family who don't bond with a human soul, but would instead—"

"Ride them like a magic pony. Yeah, I know." I loved the look of shock and confusion on their faces. "I'm not totally helpless without you two. I can find things out on my own."

"So I see," Crwys leaned forward and put his hands on the table. "Dionysus and his kind are called—"

"Leviathans," I pushed back from the table. "Look, this is nice that you decided to share this information with me, especially after you swore you were walking out, but I have things to do."

"Sit. *Down*." Crwys's voice vibrated throughout the entire shop and I was on my butt before I knew what hit me. Grey sat beside me and whined. I put my hand on her head but she was looking at Crwys as if pleading with him.

"Grey, I'm sorry, but now that I know the truth, Sam's got to know," he looked at me. "Your mother went up against Dio in one of his many hosts. And he's the reason she disappeared." He pushed the file toward me again.

Levi spoke up. "Your mom and her partner were investigating a body they fished out of Lake Borgne. Eeasel Westin, art dealer out of New York. That dealer had hired a professional thief to steal a painting from the Mississippi Museum of Art in Jackson. Apparently when she went to deliver it, she either double crossed him and he ended up in the river drained of blood or he tried to double cross her and she took her fill. Either way, a priceless painting was stolen and a man was murdered."

"Your mother had a reputation as a Tracker in the magical community, didn't she?" Crwys had me pinned with his red amber eyes. "That was her special Gift from being an Elemental, where yours is healing."

"That's all I know about her." I closed the folder. "Look, I already know this. I know it was Dionysus that hired Medbh to make my mother disappear. She wasn't killed in the line of duty, not the way I was told. She was destroyed by the Queen of Faerie in return for the soul of Dionysus's host."

Levi snapped his fingers. "That's the missing piece to all this!" He jumped out of his chair. "Crwys, that's why he's going after Medbh… to get that soul back."

It was my turn to snort. "So I learned something you didn't?"

Levi looked ecstatic but Crwys didn't. "Sam, where did you get this information?"

I suddenly felt very protective of Ina. I hadn't shared much of her with Crwys because she was the only family I had that understood what I was and embraced it. "I've done my own research."

"Where?"

"Crwys, you said we were done and you walked out on me. You bring shit in here I already found out and expect me to just drop everything and obey you?"

If it weren't for the look on his face, this next statement might have made me mad. "Of course I do. You're a woman. Women do as I say."

Levi rolled his eyes.

I came from around the table and stood inches from him. I had to look up and hoped the difference in height didn't make my look of determination look more like a stomach ache. "I…don't!"

He opened his mouth, closed it, stepped back. "Why do you smell like a dragon?"

A dragon? I thought of the leather covering on the book and what Ina said about it being covered with a dragon's wing. Dragons weren't real. That was ridiculous. But…why did he pick that particular creature to compare the smell to?

124

Levi held out his hands as he moved to us. He put a hand on my shoulder. "Sam…what's happened? I noticed the redecoration of your shop and I'm guessing it wasn't another Changeling?"

I swallowed and stepped back. I figured it might be a good idea not to let Crwys smell me again, in case he decided to search my place and find the Hammer. "Dionysus came here and tried to take Medbh. They took Ivan."

"Christ," Crwys raked his fingers through his hair. "Did you call the cops? Let them know he's been kidnapped? What in the hell would your brother want with Ivan?" He glanced at Levi.

Levi looked just as confused. "I have no idea. Did he offer to trade Ivan for Medbh's head?"

They were both looking at me. I couldn't tell them the truth. If they knew I was looking for the Hammer, they would try to help, and in Crwys's case, interfere because he and Ina did not want me using that magic. Ivan was just upstairs so concealing him wasn't going to work. I had to come up with a plan that would buy me time to figure out what I was going to do with that book.

"Ivan's upstairs. Dionysus gave him back to me."

Two shocked expressions.

"Is he okay? Are you sure it's him?" Levi asked.

"Yeah."

"So you spoke to Dionysus? You know who his host is? What do they look like?"

"It's a woman. Blond. About five ten. Very leggy. And she's got Ghouls with her."

Levi nodded. "Yeah, they like Ghouls. Once they make one they can use it like a puppet."

Crwys held up his hand for Levi to stop talking. "You have to listen to me, Sam. Dionysus is dangerous. He's a liar and he has no regard for human life, do you understand? Whatever you do, don't make deals with him," he licked his lips. "Is Dio looking for the Hammer?"

I nodded.

"Has anyone found it?"

I shook my head.

My phone rang, startling me with the buzzing against my butt. I pulled it out of my pocket. It was Ina. "Hey, it's a bad time right now."

"Sorry, but it's a bad time all around. Have you seen Arwen? Some of the others said she left the party last night and her roommate said she never came home."

"I have a few things to tell you about that one," I glanced at Crwys. He and Levi were talking in hushed voices. "But I need to do it face to face."

"Well come on over. Oh did the necklace work?"

I didn't have the heart to tell her what that necklace did. "I showed it to her…but I think it was a bad idea. She's not talking anymore."

"Damn. Can you bring it with you?"

"Sure."

She disconnected.

I chewed on my lower lip as I kept the phone to my ear as if I were still talking. I liked the idea of bringing Ivan. Then I could show Ina what happened and show her the Hammer. But come to think of it, where *was* Kyle? I hadn't seen him since I was picked up at the hospital.

I hung up and pressed his contact number. The phone rang, and went to voicemail. I hung up and texted him a message instead, telling him I was headed over to Ina's and taking Ivan with me. The mention of Ivan might actually catch his attention.

Shoving the phone into my pocket I told the two of them to wait there. Down in the basement I grabbed the all white head of Medbh, the rowen box with the necklace inside and the book. I couldn't let them see the book, so I put the rowen box and book in one of the grocery store bags I used for picking up trash and brought both of them back upstairs. Setting the bag on the steps up to my apartment, I approached the two of them and set the head on the table.

"What happened to it?" Crwys leaned in to get a better look.

"I have no idea. I was hoping maybe you two could figure that out," I held up the phone. "I have to go pick up Kyle. Ivan's upstairs sleeping after his ordeal, so I'm going to tell him where I'll be and you two, please don't bother him."

"We need to find out what happened," Levi said.

"If you want to help, take the head and find out what happened to it. Find out if she's still in there because I can't hear her." I grabbed the bag and headed up the steps as they wrapped the head up in a dishrag and headed back through the front.

Grey followed me up the stairs and growled when I set the book back on the table in front of Ivan. He looked better. Still bruised, but better. "I hate to ask this…"

He made a face. "Oh no…you want me to upload it again?"

"I think when you turn it into code, it becomes invisible. And right now, I need it invisible with Crwys and Levi snooping around. I'm heading over to Ina's for a little while; when I come back you can download it. Just stay here with Grey and rest." I looked at Grey as she sat by the stairs down. "I need you to stay here with Ivan and watch him."

Grey whined and hung her head as she slowly walked to her bed by the window and plopped down on it.

I kissed his forehead, grabbed a few things and tossed them into the bag with the necklace. I lifted my jacket off the hall tree by the stairs and headed to the back…and remembered my Jeep was still at the hospital.

EIGHTEEN

I grabbed a cab to the hospital and half ran, half walked to my Jeep. The sky still threatened rain. It tasted like rain and smelled like rain but not a drop fell. Once in my Jeep, I cranked it and stared at the hospital. Robin was in there. Dying. Expecting me to come back to him. I pulled my phone out and gave the front desk a call to ask about his condition.

His condition had worsened. Robin was in a coma and not expected to survive. He had less time than Rose had.

That was another thing I was going to have to tell Ina, that the salve we painstakingly made did no good. If anything, it might have accelerated things. I wasn't surprised. Ina and I were working against Arcane Magic. Neither of us knew what we were doing.

I drove the car to Ina's and parked in my usual spot. I didn't bother with any kind of protection on the Jeep. If it rained…well… kay sera and all that shit.

The door was open so I stepped in. I didn't see any of her students and assumed she wasn't teaching that day. "Ina?"

"I'm in the kitchen."

With the bag in tow, I meandered through the house to the large, spacious kitchen. The center table was laden with baskets of apples, pears, oranges and bananas. "Wow Ina…you getting ready for a Sabbat?"

Ina stepped in from the herb room, a basket of clipped plants in her hand. "Sam…it's October thirty-first."

Oh. Right. Crap. "I'm sorry. Between worrying about Robin and Ivan and the Changelings and Arden," I sighed as I set the bag on the counter and pulled the rowan box out of it. "I haven't even considered what day it was."

Ina set the basket next to the sink and washed her hands. "I figured Kyle would want to help out with Sabbat celebrations, and Ivan would at least want a good hot meal after his ordeal."

"I have no idea where Kyle is. I haven't seen him since the hospital. Ivan's resting with Grey." I put the box on the table a beat before something clicked in my head. It wasn't so much an epiphany as my brain looking back at what Ina just said. Ina knew Ivan was missing—I told her.

I enjoy the challenge of puzzles. Not the kind with a million cardboard pieces you put together on the dining room table, but puzzles that unlock mysteries. I always thought if I weren't a Witch I'd have been a forensic technician or a pathologist. I liked reverse engineering things. Even now as I turned to watch Ina, my brain was carefully sifting through everything that happened since that mother showed up at the shop. Actions, deeds, words, comments…especially the comments.

"What is it, Sam?" Ina grabbed a paper towel and dried her hands. "You look like you need to ask me a question."

"How…did you know Ivan was back?"

She shrugged. "You told me."

Something brushed against my personal defenses and set off a wave of internal actions for me. I sent out a *feel* to look at the perimeter. I conjured my *dex* and looked at Ina through a myriad of pentagrams of changing colors. "No. I didn't." I took a step to the right, away from the bag and the island. "What would you say if I told you the Vampire that took Ivan was Arwen?"

Ina made a confused face. "I'd say you're wrong. Arwen's not a Vampire, and she's certainly not a Leviathan. Why on earth would you say that?"

"Did you know the salve didn't work? Or was it supposed to work at all?"

"Oh Sam, I'm so sorry." Ina put the towel on the counter near her basket and braced her hand against the edge. "Why are you looking at me like that? And why on earth are all your defenses up?"

"You can see them."

"Of course I can see them. I taught you how to use them."

"When did Arwen join your group?"

Ina pursed her lips and shrugged. "I don't know. Maybe six months ago? It wasn't long after you came back from Savannah, talking about Faeries and *Alfheim*." She moved away from the cabinet and her expression shifted to worry. "Sam…what's wrong? What are you thinking?"

I was thinking it was awfully convenient for this Leviathan named Dionysus to show up here in New Orleans and join Ina's coven right after I returned with Medbh's head. I was thinking that bitch… bastard…whatever it was, had wormed its way into Ina's group to learn what it could about the head. And I was thinking Ina had no idea. Hell, she might actually be one of Arwen's Ghouls and not even know it.

And I was thinking I had one hell of an imagination.

"Sam?"

I was alone here with Ina. No one else was on the grounds. My defenses stayed in place and my *dex* kept insisting Ina was human. Not a Ghoul. Dionysus might be smart enough not to involve a Witch, but to just move on the peripheral of one. The very one related to the person who had the Faerie Queen's head. "It's been a long day. That's all."

"Well, enjoy yourself tonight. Did you bring the necklace back?"

"Yeah. It's in the box." I was also asking myself why Ina was interested in an heirloom she said she forgot she had. "The reason I asked about Arwen is because she's the one that took Ivan."

Ina's expression of surprise looked real enough. And it might be she really didn't know this. "Arwen…took Ivan? Did he say why?"

"She's looking for the Hammer. Seems she knew it was with Higgins. She mysteriously knew that Ivan could see Arcane as well, so she wanted to use him to find the book."

Ina crossed her arms over her chest. "Doesn't that sound a little odd? I mean…if this creature is from one of the Demon Realms… wouldn't they already be able to *see* an Arcane object?"

That…was a brilliant observation. One I'd come up with myself. I was a little more confident Ina hadn't been Ghouled, but it was possible she'd been deceived. "That's a very valid point."

"Eh…it's always been my thinking on the whole Arcane thing," she snapped her fingers. "Remember when you saw her in the doorway while we were talking about Ivan? I'll bet that's how she found out."

Relief washed over me. That made perfect sense. "I should have suspected something was up with her then."

"How? You had no cause to use your *dex* on her."

"Yeah but…even when I used it before, it didn't show her as being a Vampire."

Ina approached me and put her hand on my shoulder. "Leviathan. Remember, they're different. Might have to recalibrate the spell to include them."

Again, Ina was right. She made sense. But then, all through my life, she'd been there for me. Found the right questions and led me down the path to the answers.

She squeezed my shoulder. "So…tell me what happened. Oh and can you start peeling those red apples for me?" Ina turned and started pulling things out of her pantry. Flour, baking soda, sugar…I figured with all the apples she was going to make pies for tonight.

I grabbed the small white-handled knife on the counter and picked up an apple. "She said Ivan couldn't find the book and she had no idea where it was. She wanted me to find it, so I made a deal with her."

Ina stopped what she was doing. "What deal?"

"I told her I'd find the book if she healed Robin."

"Well, I'm sure she can, given she's the one that created the Changelings. But, how are you going to find the book?"

I positioned the knife on the apple and started turning it in my hand. The red peel came off in a long spiral. I used to love to sit in the kitchen and do this when I was in school. I'd come home and help Ina cook while she listened to my day. I'd ask her questions and she gave me advice. There was a comfortable nostalgia in the action.

Something…spellbinding.

"The truth is, Ivan did find the book." I continued to peel the apple, not looking at Ina at all. The spinning of the glossy red fruit held my attention even as a more no-nonsense part of me pointed to a basket of peeled apples on the counter near the stove.

Ina stepped closer. "He did? Where is it?"

"I have it." One apple finished. I set it to the side and watched it wobble a bit on the table.

"Keep peeling, Samantha. I'll need at least ten apples."

I picked out a nice fat round apple and started peeling it.

"Good. Now, tell me again where the Hammer is?"

"I have it."

"Yes, but *where* is it? Is it in your apartment? Or did you hide it? Have you told Crwys Holliard about the book?"

I hesitated as I peeled the apple. Too many questions asked at once. I wasn't sure which one to answer. So I picked the last one. "He knew about the Hammer before I did."

Ina made a frustrated noise. "I'm sure he knows about the Hammer, but did you tell him *you* had the book?"

Somewhere between answering her about Crwys and her clarifying her question I decided something was wrong. I couldn't lift my eyes from the apple I peeled and I felt as if I were back in high school, recounting my day. It was something we always did. It was Ina's ritual.

Usually I wouldn't have any problem with it. But this time, there was something niggling in the back of my head. Some strange little noise. An incessant tapping, as if someone was trying to get my attention.

"Samantha, I need you to answer my question, sweetheart."

I held the peeled apple in my left hand, the knife in my right. I didn't want to peel any more apples. There were enough peeled on the counter. My thoughts felt hazy and everything else narrowed down to just the apple and knife in my head.

Again the nagging in my mind.

Ina came up behind me and put her hands on my shoulders. "Samantha, what is it? You can tell me. You can tell me everything. You've always shared with me. Tell me if you told Crwys about the book."

"No." The answer came out before I could stop it.

"Good," she squeezed my shoulders. "Now…tell me, where is the book?"

"Uploaded."

Ina hesitated. I could feel it in her hands. Her fingers were warm. I pushed my will forward and slowly, very slowly, put the apple sideways on the table. Something else had soft control of me, of my actions, of my words, and I realized it was Ina.

She was pulling *my* strings. She'd always done this, as long as I could remember. Always asked about my day, wanted to know what I was doing, and I always felt compelled to call her and tell her.

Always.

But not this time. My need to hide Ivan was stronger. My need to keep that book away from her was stronger.

My need to…*protect*.

"I don't know what you mean by uploaded. The book was uploaded? Samantha, dear, you're going to have to help me out understanding this."

I brought the knife down across the apple, slicing it to the counter. The two halves fell to either side, exposing the one thing I needed to clear my head.

The pentagram.

A little known thing about apples to most, is the perfect star at their core. Five points. Five seeds.

Earth. Air. Fire. Water.

Spirit.

The center of this apple was blood red. So were the seeds.

I grabbed the first apple I'd peeled and cut it in half as well.

Blood red in the center.

"Sam, what are you doing?"

"There's blood in the center of these apples." I was counting on it being her blood. And it was just…gross. "You injected blood into these apples. In all the years I peeled apples for you…it finally dawned on me you never used them for pie." I straightened up and looked ahead, no longer forced by some unseen hand to look down. "You never made apple pie."

I felt her move behind me as her hands left my shoulders. I grabbed the only weapon I had—the only weapon I was ready to use—turned and shoved it into her forehead. *"Lady Darksome, your lie dispel, I make it right, your truth to tell!"*

The flat side of the apple against Ina's forehead smoked. Her eyes widened as she dropped the large knife she was about to plunge into my back. It clanged to the floor as my spell, in conjunction with the pentagram of the apple, held her in place. Her body vibrated and then slumped as her eyes closed.

I pulled the apple half away and she dropped like a house of cards to the floor.

The apple continued to smoke in my hand and I ran to the sink and threw it inside. I watched in morbid fascination as it continued to smoke, turn black and decay, until finally it was little more than ashes. I grabbed salt out of a nearby bowl, cast a handful onto the ashes and watched as they writhed until nothing remained. With shaking hands I turned the water on and washed it all away.

The shaking moved from my hands to my entire body as I used the sink to stand. I was trying to process what just happened, realizing that the woman who raised me had been using magic to control me all these years. But not just any magic.

Blood Magic.

My stomach heaved and I threw up in that same sink. Luckily I hadn't had much to eat, but the ache in my gut remained. I splashed water on my face and wiped it down with a clean towel.

Ina lay on the floor, her eyes closed, a pentagram burned into her forehead. The spell had been fast, it had been strong, and I hadn't been prepared. I approached her and grabbed the knife off the floor and tossed it into the sink as well.

In seconds my world turned upside down. And I wasn't sure what to do. Was Ina one of Arwen's Ghouls? If that were true, then it would have only been for a few months, since the Leviathan's appearance here. But I couldn't trust what Ina told me. What if that was a lie?

It had all been a lie. The reason for my mother's death…all fabricated for what?

To protect me? Or to control me?

I had to pull myself together. Arwen was waiting on me to find the book. And then she'd cure Robin. I didn't trust her, but I didn't have a choice either. I couldn't read the book. No one could read the book…

I ran into the herb room and yanked open the drawer. My mother's athame was there. I grabbed it and held it in my hand as my phone rang.

It was Kyle. "Where the hell have you been?"

"With my aunt. Wow…you all right?"

I took a deep breath and watched for any signs of life from Ina. I didn't want to touch her. "I'm okay. Look, can you head over to the hospital and keep an eye on Robin? He's in ICU."

"Yeah…sure. But…and don't yell at me…but why can't you?"

"Because I need to take care of a few things, okay? Just promise to keep an eye on him? And don't let anyone near him unless they say Blessed Be. Okay?"

"Oooh-kay. But this sounds nuts."

"I know. Please do it?"

"I promise."

I disconnected and immediately called Ivan. I told him to bring me my laptop bag and get over here. And to leave Grey in the apartment.

I started to call Crwys and stopped. No. Not yet. I had a few things I needed to do first, and then I'd call Crwys, and only if I needed him.

With my phone in my back pocket and the athame tucked into my belt, I looked around the house for something to use to tie my aunt up.

NINETEEN

Ivan tossed a Hello Kitty flash drive on the table beside the open copy of the Malleus Maleficarum. An hour had passed since Ivan arrived and downloaded the book again for me. We made sure to do it in Ivan's Mini Cooper while Ina was still unconscious. Ivan was more than shaken up when he saw Ina on the kitchen floor. I'd used some handcuffs I'd found in a drawer in the kitchen (I did not want to know why she had them) and tied her crossed ankles together with some packing twine I found in the pantry.

I had just wrapped a kitchen towel around her face when Ivan arrived.

Once I had the book in my hands again, I took it to the dining room and used my mother's athame to see the hidden type. I'd half filled a composition book with notes in that hour. "This would be a lot easier if the type would just stay visible."

Ivan leaned over my shoulder. "Is that an exorcism spell?"

"Yes it is. I haven't found any cure for a Changeling's toxin yet, so I'm going to have to trust Arwen that she'll come through."

"But that's only if you trade her this book."

I smiled up at Ivan. "Not this book," I said as I picked up the flash drive. "This book."

"I don't think I understand what you're doing."

"You don't have to, Ivan. Did you make the blank one?"

"Yeah, it's in the living room by the door in the bag." He pulled out a chair and raked his fingers through that thick hair of his. "So, what does this mean with Ina? She's not who she says she is?"

"I don't know. The reaction to my apple spell points to some kind of Arcane intervention, but my *dex* still says she's human."

"So…it is her."

"I think so. But I think she's been Ghouled by Arwen. Levi and Crwys said Leviathans can puppet their Ghouls, control them any way they want." I turned the page and held the athame over it. After rewriting a few things in the notebook, I put my pen down and the athame. "I've got one more thing for you to do."

He blinked at me. "I'm tired, Sam. This is taking a lot out of me."

"I know. And I'm sorry, but I need you to upload this book again."

To my surprise, he shook his head. "No. I can't do it. I won't."

Frustration clouded my tone. I was a woman on edge and I wasn't about to have people tell me no. Not when I was this close to destroying the thing that killed my mother and poisoned my boyfriend. "No?"

"Sam…this book. You don't see what I see. You can smell it. But I *see* it. And every time I upload it…" he wrapped his arms around his chest. "It feels like little pieces of it are left behind. Data that I can't scrub off. I feel…contaminated."

I stared at him. Really looked at him. Honestly, he looked worse now than he had when he was dumped at the shop's front door. Dark circles under his eyes hung heavy over gaunt cheeks. "I'm sorry. I keep asking a lot from you when you just discovered a new Gift."

"It's okay. Just… please don't ask me to do that again."

While he had it uploaded, Arwen couldn't sense it. Or even see it. But if Ivan couldn't do it again how else was I going to hide it? "Can…can you transmute it without uploading it?"

He winced. "I don't know."

I pushed the book toward him. "Try it."

"Turn it into what?"

"I don't know. Just…make it invisible."

Ivan chewed on his lower lip as he looked at the book. He put his hands out and I saw his eyes turn green. White bits of what looked like code—patterns of ones and zeros—covered the book until it wasn't there anymore.

I patted the table down. "Ivan…it's not there."

"I know. You told me to make it invisible."

"But I should still be able to touch it, right?"

He looked panicked as he reached out and patted the table. "Uh oh."

Shit. There was no telling what he just did to that book. But I couldn't think about it at that moment. I had to make the call to Arwen. With a hand on his shoulder, I grabbed the flash drive and slipped it into my pocket. "We'll figure it out later. I have to make a call."

"I need to take a nap," Ivan stood and pushed the chair in. "You mind if I head back to the shop?"

"Go ahead. I'm going to seal the house. Take it out of sight for now." I moved away from him and made sure Ina was still on the kitchen floor. "I think she'll be okay. Though," I grabbed up the twine and looped it around her ankles and then her wrists into a sturdy hog-tie. "I think this'll keep her here until I'm finished."

"Where's Kyle?"

"He's doing something else for me." I retrieved my phone. Ack. It was at twenty-five percent battery. I typed in the number Arwen texted me and waited.

"It's about time you called. I was getting worried. You have the book."

"Yes I do. You have the antidote for Robin?"

Arwen laughed. "Of course I do. So…where should we meet?"

"I think Ina Devonshire's place is a good place to start." I said that just to see what kind of rise I got out of Arwen.

I wasn't disappointed. "I take it she tipped her hand."

"You could say that. I don't know how long you've kept her Ghouled, but it stops tonight."

"Fine. You give me the book. I don't need her anymore."

I couldn't help but think of my mom having sought this creature out all those years ago, only to have it make a deal with the Faerie. "No Faerie deals."

"No what?"

"No. Faerie. Deals."

Arwen laughed. "Sure, Samantha. Whatever you say. But I don't think Ina's house is a good place to meet. Let's say eight o'clock, at Couturie Forest. And make sure you come alone. Oh and don't forget that beautiful necklace Ina gave you. I think it should look nice around my neck."

She disconnected before I could protest.

Why would she want to meet in a forest and not Ina's house? And what was so interesting about the necklace?

"Sam?"

I'd nearly forgotten Ivan was there. "Yeah?"

He was looking inside the bag I'd brought from the apartment. "What's all this stuff in here? Looks like things from your altar. And... what's this folder?"

Folder? I turned to see him pull the folder Levi had brought out of the bag. I'd forgotten about that thing. "Stuff about my mother. Take that back to the apartment with you okay? But leave the bag."

"Sure." He tucked the folder under his arm after he pulled his hooded jacket back on. He looked down at me with a strange expression. "Do you know what you're doing? Because Kyle and I would help you. You know that. So would Crwys."

"I realize that. But it's okay. I need to meet with Dionysus myself. Give him the book and make sure Robin's healed. Then we can all go back to the way things were."

Ivan smirked. "That's never an easy thing."

"No, it's not," I put my hand on his cheek. "Get back to the apartment and keep Grey company. I'm sure she's going nuts by herself."

I watched him leave and waited until his Cooper was out of sight before I transferred the copy of the Hammer into my bag, along with the necklace.

Ina lay perfectly still but breathed evenly. I didn't know how long the spell would keep her under, but like this she would be safe. And once I got rid of Dionysus and Robin was well...Inamorata and I were going to have a long talk.

TWENTY

Couturie Forest was part of New Orleans City Park. The park officially closed at night, but that didn't prevent kids and drug dealers from making it their home, especially this night. Halloween.

I was surprised to see the parking area off of Harrison empty. I pulled in and my ears popped as I moved through a ward I assumed had been set by Arwen. I guessed it was to keep curious eyes blind.

Once the engine was off I stepped out and cast a perimeter search around the place. My magic bounced against the barrier and made it visible to me for an instant. Ivan was right. Arcane looked like millions of writhing red worms.

I didn't find anything Vampire-like on my own magical radar so I sent a few *feels* around the area. These would pull along their connection to me when they sensed something.

I could feel the borders between the worlds thinning like they always did on this night. With my bag over my shoulder, I locked the Jeep and strode into the park.

My *feels* twigged about twenty feet in, which pretty much felt like the sound of someone's nails down a chalk board. Arwen and her people hadn't arrived by any conventional means. I was pretty sure they were here much earlier to set up a perimeter around me.

Shadows multiplied along the edges of the thick trees as an opaque fog rolled in. Nice touch.

A figure materialized in the center of the fog. It elongated and then morphed into the curves of a woman with a sexy walk. Arwen remained shadowy but it was her.

Four of her ninja Ghouls appeared, two on either side. Arwen had changed from her earlier suit into something long, flimsy and sheer. With the soft breeze from Pontchartrain moving her hair and the flimsy dress, she looked like a B-movie Goddess. She was also barefoot. I supposed this was Dionysus's attempt at his infamous theatrics.

With a firm hand on the canvas bag, I stepped forward. Once there was a sufficient distance between us, I stopped. "I have the book."

"Yes, you do." She gave me a winning smile. Arwen had chosen the perfect place to enhance her beauty, complete with a break in the trees for the moon. I could see her ruby lips and white teeth. She was as ethereal as a Vampire should be. Seductive and dangerous.

Her Ghouls moved about like liquid shadow, pouring themselves all around. They fanned out in an almost military fashion to encompass the car. "You need to tell your puppets to back off. I'm not here for tricks, Dionysus. I'm here for the antidote."

She didn't make any gesture or say anything, but the Ghouls moved away.

I reached inside the bag and pulled out the book. "This is what you want."

Arwen held out her left hand and the Ghoul closest to her placed a phone in it.

"What the fuck are you playing at?" I said.

"I have someone near your darling in the hospital. If I get the book, I tell them to administer the antidote. You didn't think I'd hand over an actual Arcane spell to an Elemental, did you? I am a God, little Witch. I'm not stupid," she brought the phone up closer to her lips. "Ginger, can you hear me?"

"Yes Mistress. I hear you," came another woman's voice from the phone's tiny speakers.

"Are you ready?"

"I would be, but there's a Witch guarding the boy."

I smiled at Kyle's heroics. "Kyle?" I raised my voice. "How many Ghouls are with you?"

"One."

Since he and I started our little fight against the Demon Realms,

Kyle and I devised certain protocols for dangerous situations. One of those protocols was if one or the other asked about the number of an enemy, we add two to a spoken numeral if we suspected more. Saying one meant Kyle saw one, but he suspected there were at least two more. "That one Ghoul is supposed to give Robin an antidote."

"Yeah that's what she said," Kyle said through the phone's tiny speaker. "But how do I know that's what that is?"

I arched my brows. "How can he tell?"

"Ginger, let the boy examine the antidote, but don't let him inject it."

We waited for a bit while mumbling and some ambient noise came through the speaker. I had no idea how Kyle was going to tell but I trusted him. I had no choice.

Then, "Hey Sam? It's good. Not a poison. I don't know if it's an antidote, but it won't kill him any different than the toxin's doing right now."

Well, that wasn't as reassuring as I'd wanted to hear, but it would have to do. "Okay. Merry meet."

Merry meet was a simple goodbye to most of the Witch community. In this situation, it was also the name of a spell he should use. A spell that would render any Ghouls nearby, immobile.

"Merry meet." And he understood.

Arwen lowered the phone. "You have your proof?"

I walked to her and stopped a few inches away and offered the book. "Just tell her to inject."

Arwen didn't take the book. The Ghoul on my right did and then held it to her chest. She closed her eyes and then nodded like an excited puppy.

Arwen seemed satisfied. She held the phone to her lips again. "Give him the antidote."

I stepped back and waited. There were a few sounds, a short grunting noise and then, "It's all good," Kyle said and I sighed with relief. The spell had been a success.

When I started to turn, she stepped forward as she handed the phone back to her Ghoul. "Wait."

I looked back at her. "Our deal's done."

"The necklace?"

Christ. "What about it?"

She held out her hand. "I want it. I saw it at Ina's and I was very upset she gave it to you," Arwen smiled. "Just think of it as…a token of trust."

Trust? Was she serious?

I reached in the bag and pulled the necklace out. I had the flash drive ready; everything I needed was in the bag. I just had to get rid of the Ghouls.

I tossed her the necklace. Arwen caught it in mid-air. "Thank you, Samantha Hawthorne, daughter of Elizabeth Hawthorne. I will admit, watching you grow up all these years under my tutelage has been somewhat satisfying. Especially since Medbh stole my host's soul. Eliza tried to hide you from me…and in the beginning I never saw the spell, it was so expertly woven into your life and your father's life. But eventually all things bend to me. Your mother bent. And so did your aunt."

I knew she was telling me this, saying these things to bait me. But why? She had what she wanted. Did she suspect my plan? Did she already know the book in her Ghoul's hand was empty of spells?

A thicker mist crawled out of the forest and covered the forest in both directions. A buzzing started in my ears and built into a thundering crescendo as something materialized out of that mist. Horse hooves pounded the asphalt as they raced toward us and then surrounded us as we stood in what felt like the eye of a storm.

In the front, seated on a white mare, flanked by men in silver armor, was the Obsidian Queen.

Brendi Ross.

The very one I'd broken a vow with. *Aw…crap.*

She held a simple black staff in one hand and the reins of her horse in the other.

Arwen approached Brendi and offered her the necklace. Brendi took it, held it up and smiled. "Yes. This will work."

I looked from Brendi to Arwen and then to Brendi. "What… what the hell's going on?"

"Samantha Hawthorne," Brendi said and her voice carried over the wind and chaos. "You have deceived the Obsidian Throne, as well as allowed the head of the former Queen to be desecrated by a Leviathan."

Then it all kicked for me. Arwen wanting to meet in the forest on Halloween night, the comments about my mother, luring me to stay. "Arwen made a deal with you, didn't she? Just like she made a deal with Medbh to get rid of my mother."

"Yes. She wishes the return of her body's soul."

Arwen laughed. "The Queen's price was Medbh's soul, which you so happily transferred into that necklace."

I felt the ground drop out from under me. "What..."

"There was one other condition to my price," Brendi smiled down at me. "You."

I did *not* see that coming.

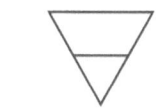

TWENTY ONE

Brendi didn't make a move. She didn't even dismount. She just ushered her horse to the edge of my shield and held out the necklace. "You made a deal with me, Samantha. You lied to me. There is a price to pay."

I put up a shield of false bravado, something I was so not feeling. "You can't touch me, Brendi. You promised your father. You pardoned me, or is the word of a Faerie worth so little now?"

"I promised my father I wouldn't hurt you. What I'm about to do won't hurt, but it will make me happy."

I didn't know what she meant. I was trapped in a circle of mist, surrounded by invisible ninja Ghouls, faced with a Leviathan and a Faerie. These were so not good odds.

Brendi held out her staff. "I sentence you to the same punishment your mother endured, Samantha Hawthorne—"

I felt the brush of her magic as it bounced against my personal wards. She was trying to force a spell on me and I wasn't about to let her. I held my arms out and summoned the four Elements, but before each of them could appear, I saw a burst of flame immediately to Brendi's right. Rider and horse were gone in an instant.

The others and their mounts, including Brendi and her own, side-shuffled away as another Faerie evaporated into flame. Again, along with their mount.

"Treachery!" Brendi said as she whirled on Arwen and pointed her staff at her. "You have deceived me!"

"No!" Arwen and her Ghouls backed up into the mist. I saw the first Ghoul ignite with a short scream and burn away to little more than floating ash. She'd been the one holding the book, which fell to the ground with a thud when she vanished.

More of them vaporized in flashes like road flares along a dark highway. All gone. Until the only one left standing was Arwen.

"Wait!" I cried out. "She killed my mother!" I looked around. I knew what was happening. I knew where the flames were coming from.

Crwys.

He walked through the mist to stand between Brendi and I. Levi sauntered up as well, dressed in black and making it look good.

"You want a war between our people?" Brendi was staring at Crwys.

"I don't have a people. I'm sure you've learned that about me by now. My family is long dead. You have your prize. I suggest you continue on with your Hunt."

"I want *her*!" She pointed her staff at me and Crwys moved himself between us.

"You know the rules, Unseelie Sidhe. One trade. One agreement. You can't claim two and you've already accepted one. Go," he took a step closer. "Or I'll burn all of you. And you know I can."

Brendi actually hissed as she pulled the reins of her horse. Her remaining contingent of helmed Faeries followed behind her as they galloped back into the mist.

But when I looked away, Arwen was gone as well.

"Dammit!" I ran to where she'd been, and where the book had fallen. The mist cleared away with the October breeze and the only thing left was small piles of ash. "She got away!"

Crwys was in my face in seconds, both his hands on my upper arm. "What the hell were you doing? Out here by yourself? Are you crazy?"

I tried to pull free but he held on tight and I kicked his shin. That made him let go as he stumbled back. I pointed at him. "Don't you ever manhandle me like that again!"

"I just saved your life!"

"I didn't ask you to!" I was breathing hard and my throat ached from screaming. My jacket felt hot and I dropped the bag as I took it off.

"Sam," Crwys took a step closer. "I tried to call you. Went by your shop and found Ivan and Grey. He told me what happened at Ina's and I'm sorry. I'm sorry she deceived you all that time."

"Ina was just a tool," I looked in the direction Arwen had been standing. "The Ghouls were a tool. And in the end I was a tool as well. All of it, just so she could get that soul back. And now Brendi's going to give it to her. And Brendi will do it because she hates me."

"Why don't we just…head back to your shop. We can take a breather and see where we are. Figure out the next step."

"There is no next step," I turned to him. "Dionysus had Medbh make my mother disappear. She robbed me of her since I was eight years old. She apparently Ghouled Ina when I was young and she's been spying on me all this time. My life is a lie…" I put my hands to my face. "And she got away with it. I'm supposed to fight for justice and I can't even win it for myself."

Crwys put his hand on my back. I felt the heat of it through my shirt and pulled away.

"Sam…please…let's go back to your place. Is Robin okay?"

"Robin's fine!" I shouted, grabbed my bag and headed back to my Jeep. "Go on back to the shop. I need to go see him."

The two of them followed close behind me as I tossed my bag in and cranked the Jeep.

"Maybe I should come with you?" Crwys looked like a little boy standing outside.

"No. I just…I need some time to think, okay? I want to see Robin." I knew on some level my saying I needed to see Robin hurt Crwys. But he was a big boy and took it well enough. He stepped back and I hauled ass out of the parking lot and onto Harrison.

But I didn't go to the hospital.

I headed to Ina's.

It was the one place I was sure Arwen would show up.

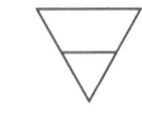

TWENTY TWO

I was still shaking when I parked the Jeep in its usual spot in front of Ina's. The house looked well lit from the road, but the barrier to keep it invisible to the Cowens was in full force as kids of all ages dressed in costumes, some home made, some store bought, ran back and forth along the sidewalk, visiting the huge houses with their expensive candy.

The air still smelled of rain as I grabbed my guns and tucked them into my back pockets. I took the bag and headed through the gate and up the walkway.

The closer I got to the house, the more on edge I became. Something was inside, and I was damn sure it wasn't Ina. The fact I'd left her there trussed up and helpless didn't help my anxiety as I tried the door. Finding it open, I pushed it in but stood at the threshold.

The lights were on, just as I'd left them. Nothing stirred. I pulled a gun from my back pocket with my right hand and thumbed the hammer back. Holding it with the barrel pointed up, I stepped inside. Again, my ears popped like they had when I stepped into the woods.

My boots were silent on the hardwood floor as I moved into the main room, then into the TV room. I saw movement in the kitchen and slipped to the side to look around the corner.

Arwen was there, stirring something on the stove. Ina was tied to one of the dining room chairs, a blindfold over her face. She struggled now and then but didn't make a sound.

"Come on in, Samantha," Arwen said, but didn't turn to face me. "I've been expecting you."

I stepped in and pointed the gun at Arwen. "Turn around real slow. I don't think a simple bullet can hurt you—"

"No, but the magic you infuse your weapons with might do a bit of damage. After all, that is why you couldn't tell what I was," she half turned from her waist and smiled at me. "You did realize that, didn't you? Thanks to Medbh, for all intents and purposes I'm human."

Dammit. That's right. The *dex* wouldn't see Arwen as a Leviathan or a Vampire because it would detect a single soul. Not the dual souls. I made an internal groan at my stupidity. "Step away from the stove."

"Why? I'm heating up some soup. I'm sure Ina's hungry, and a bit uncomfortable, after you just left her on the floor like that. So naughty." Arwen moved the pot off of the stove and set it on the counter to her left. She picked up a towel and wiped her hands before she turned and faced me. "So…I see I was betrayed again by a damn Faerie."

"If you mean Brendi not taking me, that's because the rules wouldn't allow her to. One deal, one payment. Getting Medbh *and* me constituted two."

Arwen nodded. "And she'd already accepted Medbh. Makes sense. So…where's your demon lover? The one that so swiftly destroyed nearly all my Ghouls?"

"He's not my lover and I don't know if he's a demon."

"Sweetheart," Arwen lowered her shoulders. "He torched how many people in those woods? I'd call that little talent demon worthy. But it doesn't matter. I still get my wish. And soon, I'll have a soul." She glanced at Ina.

Oh like 'effing hell! I moved to put myself between Ina and Arwen. "You're not taking Ina's soul."

"I'm afraid I am. See…you're under the delusion you have power here. But you don't. Nothing is going to stop the Obsidian Queen once she casts the spell. That will happen at midnight. Or it would have if you hadn't given me an empty book." She turned and moved out of the kitchen.

"Stop where you are!"

"Don't you want to come see the Circle? It's all been prepared." She kept walking through the dining room to the back sliding doors. I glanced at Ina before I followed behind Arwen. The back door was open and I stepped out into the cool evening. The Circle had been made ready, with a roaring bale fire. An altar sat in the southern quarter instead of the north. All the Elements were present.

Arwen walked into the Circle and stood before the fire. The full moon parted the clouds overhead and I checked my watch. Eleven thirty. I kept my gun up, pointed at her, as I walked around the proper opening of the Circle. "Get out of there. Now."

"Or what? You'll shoot me?" She laughed and twirled, which made the flimsy dress she still wore fly out around her. "Don't you want to know the truth, Samantha? About what happened to your mother?"

"You hired Medbh to kill her."

Arwen laughed. "I did no such thing. I made a deal with Medbh to get rid of her. Whatever that bat shit crazy bitch did was up to her. She was something else during that time. Your mother, I mean. She was tough. A real heroine. And she was good with magic. There are a lot of Vampires out there that feared her. A lot of creatures you don't even know about yet that still say her name and tremble. The fact she was able to track me down, discover who and what I was is testament to her power. And to her Gift as a Tracker. When we learned she had a daughter…well…rumor spread you were just like her."

I moved into the Circle, but didn't feel the usual pressure against my skin. There was no Circle cut in this space. No sacred ground consecrated. "You can stop now."

"But I want you to know the truth, Samantha. How your mother tried to kill me in a Circle just like this one," she held out her arms. "But she failed the first time because she didn't have the power. She didn't have the Arcane spell necessary to exorcise me. So she went in search of that spell, found it with the help of a dear, close friend who was married to the local High Witch. They made an agreement that just this once they would learn Elemental Arcane."

"My mother never used Arcane."

"No. But she knew it. She practiced it. And she would have been good at it if she'd been allowed to continue. Eighteen years ago, this very night, her coven dragged me into a Circle and waited on their precious Elizabeth to come and destroy me," Arwen smiled and the moonlight cast her face in deep shadows. "But she never did. Poor Eliza. She was never seen or heard from again. And what to do about that lovely child and grieving husband she left behind?"

"Stop it."

"Aww… does it bring back bad memories for the little Sam? So alone now with no mommy?"

"Shut the fuck up."

"Hard to hear, isn't it? That while you all believed, by a spell no less, that she'd died in the line of duty, I escaped those weaker Witches and killed all but one. The very one that gave your mother the spell to destroy me."

I already knew she was talking about Inamorata.

"So I made sure you were raised right, not knowing what you were capable of, learning only what I wanted you to learn and sticking to just the basics. Hell, little Sammie, I even made sure you had a tender spot in your heart for Vampires. And it paid off. You've let a few of them live. Your mama wouldn't have done that."

I fired. I wasn't sure I meant to but I was angry and I wanted her to stop. The bullet hit her shoulder and spun her to the left. She fell and looked like a downed damsel in distress in the grass.

And she was laughing. Just…*laughing*.

I rushed to her and fired again…and again. One bullet hit the ground near her head and the other hit her in the thigh. She was bleeding and laughing at me.

There was only one way to stop this. One way to prevent her and Brendi from sacrificing Ina's soul. I turned to the altar and started to set my gun on it—but I couldn't. I couldn't let an instrument of death touch a sacred altar. I dropped it to the ground and kicked it under the altar as I pulled the Hello Kitty flash drive from my pocket and slammed it on the altar's surface.

The thing exploded in a sparkling light of yellow and red as it projected the pages I'd written out of the book. I put myself into a slight trance as I read the instructions.

"What…what are you doing?" Panic now flooded Arwen's voice.

I lit a small briquette of charcoal and sprinkled Frankincense over it. I lifted the long knife sitting by the Fire candle so she could see it in the moonlight and sprinkled salt over its hilt. "I'm going to finish what my mother started, Dionysus. I'm going to rip your soul from that body so hard it won't survive the trip to the Well of Souls."

I passed the blade through the smoke that swirled into the air.

"You can't do that! You're using Arcane! Witches can't use Arcane!"

I ran the blade through the flame of the red candle on the altar. "Witches are told they shouldn't use it, because it will leave scars on them, marks that could cause bad things to happen to them."

"And you'd risk that? To exorcise me? I didn't do anything to your mother! That was Medbh."

I then held the blade out as I poured water over it and let the excess spill on the grass. I didn't answer her this time. I didn't have anything to say. The blade was now consecrated by the Elements and infused with my will as it glowed a soft blue and white. All I had to do now was set the symbols. Ten of them. I had them all memorized.

I approached Arwen who tried to move away. But she was sluggish and weak with the loss of blood. A normal human would have passed out from the loss of blood. But not a monster like this, keeping the body alive while it fought to live.

The gown she wore, the silk now hardened with dried blood, exposed her arms from the shoulders. Her skin was as pale as the moon above us. There was very little blood as I carved the first symbol into her flesh with the knife.

She struggled harder and managed to wrench her arm from my grip. I got it back again and this time shoved her down on her side with her carved arm up. I managed the second, then the third, fourth and fifth symbol as she struggled. Running out of arm room, I moved the point of the blade to whatever bare patch of flesh I could find as I carved the next five symbols. She screamed and yelled, but I forced all of my will, all of my power into making the symbols just right. No one could hear her because nothing could get past the barrier on the house.

When I was done, I sat back and held the knife up over my head. Lightning flashed across the sky, followed by thick, loud thunder. Was it finally going to rain?

"No!" Arwen screamed as she put up a hand.

I spoke the words of the spell as I plunged the knife through her ribcage and into her heart where her foul, demonic spirit was fused.

Arwen writhed and kicked with the knife sticking from her chest. Only the hilt was visible. Blood seeped over the Circle grass. It hissed and smoked where it touched the earth. Her mouth opened wide as her chest arched and she nearly levitated. Thunder shook the ground beneath me as the Leviathan finally collapsed. Her open eyes stared at the sky as it opened up and rain came down in large, cold drops.

I sat close by as the rain fell, plastering my hair to my head, washing the blood away from my hands, my face, everywhere it had touched me. The fire sizzled and finally went out as the pit filled with water. I half crawled, half stumbled into a standing position as I moved out of the Circle and back into the house. I dripped water over the floor and mud from my boots as I moved around the dining room table and into the kitchen. It was time to free Ina and see if I had any energy left to heal what Dionysus and done.

But the chair was empty.

I picked up the handcuffs and held them out as I slowly looked around the kitchen. The house was eerily quiet, except for the tapping noises as water dripped from my hair and jacket.

"I think," came a familiar voice behind me. "Thanks are in order. It took long enough, but I'm finally free."

TWENTY THREE

Ina stood in the doorway from the kitchen to the herb room. Her hair was down around her shoulders and gave off a radiant glow. She looked beautiful...except for the pentagram in the center of her forehead.

She looked up, almost cross-eyed, when she realized what I was looking at. "Yes. I have you to thank for it."

I stood in the middle of the kitchen, dripping, unsure what had happened. "Are...are you free of him? Of Dionysus?"

Ina laughed. "Am I free of him? I'll never be free of him," she approached me, her hand out to touch my face. "And I'll never be free of this body because of the mark on my head. But I think if I drown your in blood, I could eventually make it fade enough to do the trick." She moved her hand from my face to my hair. "You still don't see it, do you?"

I did see it.

Too late.

She grabbed a hunk of my hair and yanked me backward seconds before she sunk a knife into my stomach. Ina stepped back and smiled as her eyes turned black, and I saw her teeth. Her long, sharp teeth.

"You...escaped into Ina..."

"You can't be that dense, Samantha," her dual toned voice said. "I've been inside Inamorata all along."

I flailed as I tried to stay upright. I grabbed at the center island with its apples, but I didn't have the strength and collapsed in a heap on the floor. I put my hands to my middle and felt the knife still buried deep. I didn't dare remove it fearing I'd bleed even faster. I was dying fast enough as it was.

Ina knelt beside me and ran her long tongue against my cheek seconds before she sank her sharp teeth into my neck and drank. I moaned at the pain, but it seemed like such a little thing when weighed against the agony in my gut. She pulled away but whispered into my ear. "So easily manipulated. Since you were a child I've been there. And your mother knew I was there but there was nothing she could do about it."

I turned my head and spit blood. "Mom…" I tried to gather my power, called on the Elements one by one, but I'd exhausted myself in the Circle.

Ina grabbed my shoulders and pulled me into a sitting position. My head lolled around as my strength left my body and made garish, scarlet puddles on the ground. "Arwen was my puppet all this time… and you never even suspected." She smiled. Blood coated her teeth and lips. My blood. "And she would serve as my soul. Don't you see? You ripped the soul out of an innocent and gave it to me. Now I have a fresh soul—one I can ride wherever I want to go, and it's all because of you!"

My own soul felt nauseous for what I'd just done. I literally just murdered an innocent human. And now I was dying. Was this the punishment of Arcane? Was this *my* punishment? That I would die at the hands of my mother's enemy?

She moved behind me and propped me up against her front, her breasts a cushion for my neck. "There, there, Samantha. Your purpose is done. You were to be my salvation. And you did your job perfectly. Now, I'm going to drink what's left, and then I'm going to leave. First, I think I'll Ghoul that cute little Cyber Witch of yours, the one that uploaded the book? That's a nice trick, don't you think? Yes I heard every word the two of you said. He'll be my next servant so I can use his power. And then I want a crack at that little Hedge Witch. He could be a very nice Major Domo.

"Oh…and then I need to do something about that damn fire

breather. You do realize he's in love with you, and his kind doesn't love often, and they don't let go either. He's going to cause a lot of—"

Something shook the house. I thought at first it was Ina moving, until she literally disappeared and I fell backward. I stared at the ceiling as my thoughts meandered in and out of where I was. There were spots on the white speckled ceiling. They looked like grease spots.

And who was yelling?

I could hear all kinds of yelling. Something vibrated beneath me again and I slowly blinked as the edges of my world turned black as if burning inward.

Something wet licked my face. I heard Grey whimper and saw her staring down at me, her tongue hanging out and her fur coated in Vampire blood. "You need to wash that off," I said, slurring my words. "Don't want no Ghoul doggie."

A man laughed and I looked to my left. Crwys was looking down at me and there was something really weird about him. He had this red and yellow glow all over his body. He put a hand to my cheek and his eyes looked…gold. "Trust me when I tell you Grey is incapable of that kind of transformation. Now, I need you to keep quiet."

I think I smiled. I wasn't sure if I was really doing anything. I wasn't even sure Crwys and Grey were actually there.

"Hey Crwys, it's gonna take an ambulance twenty minutes to get here and she looks bad. You want me to…you know…"

I recognized Levi's voice but I couldn't see him.

"No. I can handle Samantha."

Handle me? Ha…nobody could handle me!

Not even me.

I felt his arms beneath me and then I wasn't on the cool kitchen floor anymore. I was in the air and I was warm. So very, very warm.

I'm proud of you, baby girl.

I closed my eyes as I became weightless and just too damn tired.

"Thanks mom," I said, or I think I said it, before I drifted off into a nice red amber dream.

TWENTY FOUR

I heard voices at first. Lots of them. Laughter. Then some smells that made me scrunch my nose. Something soft brushed my cheek and I batted at it. Damn flies.

"I think she's finally coming back to the land of the living," Kyle said.

I opened my eyes to look into his brown ones. He was way too close and I put my hand on his face and pushed him away. "Personal space, dude."

"Oh, she's fine," Ivan said and he appeared behind Kyle. He looked as adorable as ever and waved. "Welcome back."

Just past Ivan was a flat screen TV on the wall. I recognized the show but couldn't remember ever putting a TV in my bedroom.

I wasn't in my bedroom.

"Aw no…a hospital?" I blinked several times to look around and yeah, it was a hospital room. Semi-private. A curtain separated me and some other poor schmoe. I touched my stomach but it was wrapped really, really well. "I'm assuming I survived my first stabbing?"

"Yeah. It looks pretty good considering. And you survived a pretty nasty Vampire bite, but I wouldn't go telling the nurses that's what's on your neck," Kyle put his hand on the side railing. "You lost a lot of blood."

"Yeah, that's what happens when you fight a Leviathan," I looked around again. "Where are Crwys and Levi?"

"On the job." Ivan shoved his hands into his pockets. He looked sad. "It didn't work, did it?"

Oh, it worked. I just didn't know if he knew it worked on the wrong person. I shook my head before I cleared my throat. "Did Inamorata…"

"She got away," Kyle said. "I'm so, so sorry, Sam. We didn't know."

"None of us did," Ivan looked really upset. "And what she did to Arwen…did you get there before she did that or did Dionysus do that after she stabbed you?"

I didn't say anything.

Kyle spoke up. "Come on. Fill us in. 'Cause Detectives Vague and Whut had no idea. Crwys thinks you got there after Dionysus had already killed Arwen. I mean…you tried to stop her and that's the best you could do."

I still didn't say anything. I should, I knew that. I should tell them the truth. Tell them *I* was the one that killed her. *I* was the one that used Arcane. *I* was the one Dionysus tricked into doing his dirty work.

Kyle and Ivan continued talking, and I didn't…say…a word.

Kyle held out his finger at me. "I know about you translating that Arcane stuff. Just be glad you didn't do any of it, okay? You need to rest and you need to heal," he moved back. "Sam, don't let this get you down. We'll catch her. Him. The Leviathan. And we'll banish it the right way, okay? You've got me and Ivan, and Crwys and Levi are willing to help. Oh and Grey…she's already chewed a hole in your couch."

I forced a smile. "Thanks for taking care of her."

"Seven days," Ivan said. "You've been in here seven days. Just so you know."

My jaw dropped. Seven days? I made an internal sigh. That meant Dionysus could be anywhere by now. And luckily she hadn't touched Ivan. Or Kyle. I needed to talk to Crwys and find out what happened while I lay on the floor bleeding to death.

Ivan stepped to the curtain. "So, you want to meet your roommate?"

"Sure?"

Ivan pulled the curtain back.

Robin sat on the edge of the other bed, wearing a red flannel robe, looking as beautiful and awesome as ever. He stood with help from Ivan and made his way to me where he leaned over and gave me a big kiss. He was alive and healthy and warm next to me.

I thought of Arwen's body on the ground, dead in the rain, and her soul now owned by Dionysus.

At some point the other two left the room, but I didn't notice until Robin kissed my nose. "A Vampire, huh?"

"Mmhmm."

"Downloading magic files?"

"Mmhmm."

"And exorcising demons."

"All in a day's work."

He nuzzled next to me. "You better get overtime for this."

TWENTY FIVE

In the aftermath, and there was always aftermath, the insurance rejected the claim on the window. And the company I ordered a lot of the destroyed product from also refused to take my claim. They wanted to be paid for the order, even though I didn't have it to sell to get them the money.

A month after Dionysus escaped, I stood by the computer in the shop, surfing the Internet for cheaper digs. The way things were going, and the drain on my bank account, made it impossible to keep the doors open. I was facing the loss of everything I'd worked for.

I'd asked Ivan and Kyle to take a few days unpaid after Thanksgiving so I could sort out my next step. Robin was busy getting his remaining niece settled in with his parents in Gulfport. No one had found the missing children yet, and I suspected they were somewhere in *Alfheim*. I planned on asking the Silver Queen if she knew their whereabouts. I didn't want to give Brendi any ideas about trading their safety for my head.

Tourists moved back and forth outside, but no one stepped into *Bell, Book and Candle.*

Not with that huge foreclosure sign tacked to the window.

I'd talked to Crwys and Levi together and separate after I was released from the hospital, to find out what happened. And they told the same story. They got Ina's address from Kyle, who was worried because I hadn't returned his call. When they got there, they found me bleeding and Ina about to bite me.

The two of them fought the old bitch, who was very spritely for her age. Something happened and she was gone.

I couldn't help the feeling that something was a something they didn't want to tell me, just like I had a few somethings I didn't want to go into either. So, I left it alone and moved on as best as I could.

The foreclosure was taking up a lot of my extra thinking time.

When the bell over the door jingled, I looked away from the monitor to see Crwys step in. He wore his usual leather jacket, jeans, sneakers and smarmy smirk. When he stopped just inside and yanked the notice off the door window, I slipped off the stool. "Hey…you can't do that."

"Yeah I can. Because it's not happening."

Grey stood up and made her way from behind the counter to receive her greeting from Crwys. "You want to explain that?"

"Sit down. And I need you to listen to me."

Grey returned to me and took up her position on her huge pillow behind the counter as I hopped on the stool. "What?"

"You know I'm not human."

"Right."

"And you've probably guessed I'm long lived."

"Yeah."

"So, it shouldn't surprise you to know I'm not financially strapped."

I didn't say anything because I wasn't sure what he was saying.

"I had a little business to take care of this morning. I like this place. And I like you, even if you keep pushing me away." He leaned on the counter in front of me. I noticed a new ring. A silver dragon with a red ruby eye. "I want to help and I knew you'd never let me."

I blinked at him. "What did you do?"

"I paid the debt. There's a repair crew coming in this afternoon to get this place in shape and you have a new duplicate shipment of whatever it is you sell coming in tomorrow. So in three days, you'll be back in business, just in time for the Christmas shopping rush to begin."

I opened my mouth to protest. Yeah I was appreciative and yeah I was trying not to climb over the counter and hug him but—

Crwys held up his hand. "The only thing I want, Samantha, is to be a silent partner in the business. I won't take a salary. I won't ask to see records. I just want you to stay open. And if you keep doing the good work you're doing, this place is going to get dinged up again and again. So, my payback for you is to keep it running smooth. Okay?"

I stared at him. At his red amber eyes. His dark lashes. His full lips. I'd thrown this man out of my life twice, but he was still here. "No strings?"

"No strings."

I held out my hand and we shook on it. I hoped he didn't feel the guilt that still wrapped around my heart, a little tighter every day. I hadn't come clean about Arwen's death. I was afraid to let them know I was the one that murdered her. I'd carved her up in cold blood and stabbed her through the heart, tossing her soul into the open mouth of a demon.

I didn't know if this was my punishment for using Arcane, or if there was something else to come.

But Dionysus was still alive and one day I'd see him again. And I would need to be ready.

The door burst open and a young kid, maybe fourteen, ran in. He stopped in the center of the shop, spotted us and pointed. "I need a love spell!"

Crwys chuckled, patted the counter and stepped away. "Get back to work, Hawthorne. Save the world."

For the first chapter of Elemental Shadows…

ELEMENTAL SHADOWS
CHAPTER ONE

"You can't possibly understand what I'm going through."

"Sweet Lord and Lady, Robin. You think I've never lost anyone before? What about Ina? What about my mom?"

"It's not the same. You didn't *kill* them." Robin turned as he braced himself against the break room sink. He hung his head. "You've never killed anybody. Not like I killed Kathy."

To anyone coming into this conversation, this wasn't a murder confession. Robin Tremere didn't murder a person—he killed a Changeling, a creature made of Arcane Faerie Magic. That Changeling had taken the place of his niece Kathy, killed her mother, Robin's sister, and nearly killed him. He would have died if I hadn't made a deal with a Leviathan named Dionysus.

But Robin didn't know any of those details. I didn't believe he was ready to know. I'd kept it all hidden within the Witch's world of magic and secrets, in the shadows of reality that permeated New Orleans. It's not that I meant to sound cryptic; it's just that sometimes secrets are necessary.

Like *my* secret. The one where I did kill someone. An innocent. And I used forbidden magic to do it.

And who am I? Samantha Hawthorne, Elemental Witch and said wielder of bad joojoo. Robin and I were in my magic and herb shop, *Bell, Book and Candle*, a little place on Bourbon Street where I lived and worked, saved the world from evil, and sometimes made a small profit to buy food. Two weeks had passed since the incident with the Changelings and Dionysus. The twelve original children the little monsters were created from were still missing, despite my efforts to find them, along with any in the magical community with the ability to Track.

I didn't think telling Robin that Kathy might still be alive was a good idea. I didn't want to give him false hope because I feared Kathy and the other missing children were in *Alfheim*, the Faerie Realm, and if they ate or drank anything, or were favored by the Obsidian Queen, they were probably already transformed into whatever she considered appropriate.

This was just my own worse case scenario. I should have already contacted one of the two Queens, either the Obsidian, Brendi, or the Silver, Tzariene. Winter and Summer. But I had made a deal with the Winter Queen, Brendi, and then reneged on it. The only thing that kept her from taking me and turning me into a horse or a toad or something much worse (I'd been transformed into a stone fountain before so I knew there was a *much worse*) was the Queen's father, who had asked Brendi to forgive me.

She did, but I always feared my deal wasn't as much forgotten as placed in a weird sort of forbearance. I mean…she'd tried to make a deal with Dionysus to trade me for a soul. The only that thing that stopped Brendi then was a technicality, which I was damn sure did nothing to soften our relationship.

 Robin was the one I was worried about now. Having lost his sister so fast, knowing it was his hand that killed his "niece," and now suddenly taking on the role of uncle—it was too much on his shoulders. He looked thinner, paler, and I noticed the dark circles under his eyes deepening with every day.

He'd come to ask if I could make him a tea or a spell or something that would stop him from feeling.

And that was something I just wouldn't do.

I stood from my chair at the break room table, a large oak handmade work of art, and took my empty mug with me. Robin still had his head bent and he was white-knuckling the marble edge of the sink. I put a hand on his back and rubbed it. "Robin, I'll agree I don't understand what you're feeling. But what I can speak to is the necessity of working through raw emotions. If we never feel or endure hardships, then we never learn from them."

"That's so easy for you to say," his voice was low but his blond hair obscured his face. "You who have all this power, all these things you can do." Robin put his hands to his sides and straightened. The face he turned to me wasn't a nice one. In fact, it wasn't a face I'd ever seen him wear. "Make me forget."

"No."

"But you can do it."

"No. I can't." It was a lie. But it was one of those good lies. It just felt…wrong.

"Then I'm just wasting my time with you." His voice sliced into my heart as he stalked out of the break room, through the door to the shop.

I followed him, calling after him like some lovesick girl. Which in truth I was. "Robin, wait…please!"

Two customers turned to watch us, probably thrilled to have some kind of drama interrupt their morning. I could feel Kyle's eyes on me. He was at the tarot table, helping one of those customers. Kyle Kendrick was my oldest friend and my partner in the store.

"Don't talk to me!" Robin shouted as he yanked open the front door. He turned to look at me. I came to an abrupt stop in front of him, my eyes wide and not liking this side of him. Or this pitiful side of me. "You can help me, but you *won't*. You think my suffering is some kind of noble thing, don't you? Well you can take your magic shit and—"

He didn't finish his sentence and for a half second, I was glad.

But then that half second stretched into a full minute and I realized Robin wasn't moving. His mouth was open in mid-insult, and he wasn't blinking.

"What the hell?"

I turned at the sound of Kyle's voice and noticed the other two customers weren't moving either. Kyle waved his hand in front of the face of the one he was helping.

Nothing.

"This doesn't bode well."

I moved away from Robin toward the counter where I kept my weapons during the day. I couldn't shake the feeling something was crawling up my back, under my shirt. Kyle was right—having Cowens (non-witches) freeze like this inside my own store, within my own wards, was not going to bode well at all. Something was coming.

With a slight surge of my own power I summoned a Fire Elemental, a Salamander, my favorite of the Elemental creatures. My hands should have glowed with transparent red fire.

But they didn't.

Not a single Salamander appeared.

I tried again with a Gnome for Earth, then an Undine for Water. Still nothing.

So I summoned the element of Air, and to my surprise a small, white swirling image appeared in front of me as Kyle moved in close. I could clearly see the Sylph's face as he stretched his arms and yawned.

"Haven't been using that Element a lot, huh?" Kyle said, indicating the creature's perceived lethargy.

"Shush." I focused my attention on the Sylph who nodded and pointed to the door. With an abrupt clarity and swiftness, I saw an aerial image of four black-clad individuals moving through Bourbon Street without the slightest odd look from tourists or natives. Cloaks billowed out behind them in slow motion and I asked the Sylph to change positions so I could see them from the front.

My skin grew cold and this time it was me white-knuckling the counter before I reached down and retrieved one of my Smith & Wessons.

"What?" Kyle asked to my left. "What is it? I can sense something's coming but I can't see it."

"Yeah," I said as I pulled away from the Sylph's vision and asked the Elemental to stay and witness. He agreed and moved to settle atop one of the crystal balls on the far left shelf. My hands glowed yellow as I lifted the pistol with the name The Lady engraved on its barrel. "We got company all right. Get in the back and fire up your best defense spell."

"What?" But he was moving back to the door to the break room.

Robin and the two customers abruptly turned toward the front in unison, and filed out of the shop without a backwards glance.

I checked my ammo, cocked my wrist so the cylinder would snap back and held the now yellow fiery gun in my hand. I knew what was coming, and Kyle had been right. "Clerics."

This did not bode well.

* * *

Check out Elemental Shadows at your favorite retailer!

Thank you for purchasing and reading Elemental Arcane. It would be greatly appreciated if you could take a moment and leave an honest review of this book within the guidelines of your favorite retailer. Reviews help authors qualify for advertising and promos, which translates into savings for the readers.

If you want to be notified when Phaedra's next novel is released and get free stories and occasional other goodies, please sign up for her mailing list at her website at phaedraweldon dot com.

Your email address will never be shared and you can unsubscribe at any time.

GLOSSARY

Pronunciations:
Crwys - *Cruise*
Medbh - *Mayv*
Sidhe - *Shee*
Dijin - *Gin*
Alfheim - *Alf-hime*

Definitions:

Magical Parliament - a grouping of 13 High Witches chosen from all over the world to regulate magic use and the teaching of magic so as to avoid revealing a Witch's presence to the Cowen world. There are more than 13 High Witches at any given time, but only 13 are chosen to serve in Parliament.

Demon Realms - worlds that exist outside and yet beside the Material Plane. Other names used for these realms are the Mental, Astral, Abysmal, Ethereal, Peripheral, and sometimes Alfheim.

Mother's Tracker - The Parliament once granted tracking rights to some Elder Witches, especially those with Elemental Gifts. The last Tracker to officially receive this right was Samantha's mother, Elizabeth Hawthorne. The right gave them the ability to see, hear, taste, and smell trails left behind by a named target. This is the magic Eliza used to track Dionysus and made it impossible for the Leviathan to escape Eliza's abilities.

Elemental Witch - A God Mother's child who possess all five of the Elemental Gifts; Earth, Air, Water, Fire and Spirit. The combination of the Elements make the use of Spirit possible, though small instances can be achieved with little training. Elementals use their own energy to power their magic as they transmute the magic inherent in the Material Plane into power.

Dianic Witch - A God Mother's child who does not possess any of the Elemental Gifts. Dianics are given Gifts such as second sight, telekinesis, telepathy, aural visions, clairvoyance and psychometry.

Elder Witch - A title given to any Witch possessing three Gifts, one usually required to be Elemental, who serves on the local counsels under a High Witch.

Magical Sight/Other Sight - the ability to see magic. All Witches possess this ability, but not all Cowens do. Those that can are usually slightly touched with a Dianic Gift.

Circle - Cutting the Circle is the Witch's ability to cut a circle into the Earth, thus creating sacred space for ritual.

Drawing Down the Moon - The ability of a Witch to join with the God Mother through Her blood in their veins. The phrase is also used by Dianic Witches when referring to creating sacred space.

Hierarchy:
Cowens – Non-magical folk.

Dianic Witches - God Mother's children possessing only Dianic gifts, such as telekinesis and psychometry.

Hedge Witch - God Mother's children whose Gifts contain an inherent, working knowledge of all of the Gaia's plants. They possess a very latent touch of all the Elements but not enough to wield them. They generate their magic through these combinations of herbs.

Elemental Witches - God Mother's children who possess all five of the Elemental Gifts.

Elder Witch - God Mother's children who possess at least one Elemental Gift but have dedicated themselves to their craft and their fellow Witches for the betterment of all of the God Mother's children.

High Witch - A position voted upon; a position of leadership, and not one to take lightly. In order to be a High Witch, a God Mother's child must have at least two of the Elemental Gifts and one Dianic.

Cyber Witch - Unknown.

About the Author...

Phaedra Weldon is a writer and mother of one. Born in Pensacola, Florida, Phaedra was raised in the lush, green southern tropic of Georgia. She grew up on southern ghost stories told while eating marshmallows around campfires, or on the back of pick-up trucks in the middle of cornfields on chilly October nights. Phaedra currently lives in the South with her daughter.